A SOLDIER'S WISH

The Christmas Angel Series

N.R. WALKER

Copyright

Cover Artist: Meredith Russel
Editor: Boho Edits
Publisher: BlueHeart Press

First Edition 2018

Warning

Intended for an 18+ audience only. This book contains material that maybe offensive to some and is intended for a mature, adult audience. It contains graphic language, explicit sexual content, and adult situations.

BLURB

The year is 1969...

Gary Fairchild is proud to be a hippie college student, and he protests the Vietnam War because he believes in love and peace. To him, it isn't just a counterculture movement —it's a way of life. When tickets to the Aquarium Exposition—3 Days of Peace & Music, or Woodstock, as it was better known, go on sale, there's no way he isn't going.

Richard Ronsman is a sheltered farm boy who lives in the shadow of his overbearing father. He's hidden his darkest secret to earn his father's love, but nothing is ever good enough—not even volunteering for the Vietnam War. And with just a few days left before he's deployed, he's invited by a striking hippie to join him at a music festival.

Three days of music, drugs, rain, mud, and love forged a bond between these two very different men that would shape the rest of their lives. They share dreams and fears, and when Richard is shipped off to war, they share letters and love. For Richard's first Christmas home, he is gifted a special angel ornament that just might make a soldier's wish come true.

This story is one of seven stories which can all be read and enjoyed in any order.

In 1750, a master woodcarver poured all his unrequited love, passion, and longing into his masterpiece—a gorgeous Christmas angel for his beloved's tree. When the man he loved tossed the angel away without a second thought, a miracle happened. The angel was found by another who brought the woodcarver True Love.

Since then, the angel has been passed down, sold, lost and found, but its magic remains. Read the romances inspired by (and perhaps nudged along by) the Christmas angel through the years. Whether it's the 1750's England (Eli Easton's **Christmas Angel**), 1880's New York (Kim Fielding's **Summerfield's Angel**), the turn-of-the-century (Jordan L. Hawk's **Magician's Angel**), World War II (L.A. Witt's **Christmas Homecoming**), Vietnam-era (N.R. Walker's **Soldier's Wish**), the 1990's (Anyta Sunday's **Shrewd Angel**), or 2018 (RJ Scott's **Christmas Prince**), the Christmas angel has a way of landing on the trees of lonely men who need its blessing for a very Merry Christmas and forever HEA.

A *Soldier's* WISH

N.R. WALKER

CHAPTER ONE

GARY FAIRCHILD

Thursday, August 14, 1969

"PULL IN AT THE DINER," Pauly cried.

"Man, you should've eaten already. We've only been on the road for an hour," Kathryn said. That was true. We'd left Western Connecticut State College at sunrise and had only made it as far as the prime farming country of Middletown, New York. She waved over the bench seat to the back of the van, where Pauly and I were sitting. "Check the cooler. There's plenty to eat now that Colleen isn't coming."

"Nah, I want something fried. Like eggs. And toast. And coffee," Pauly added. "And I'm pretty sure we won't be eating real food for the next three days."

I conceded with a nod. "True."

Lyman gave Kathryn a mellow smile. "The man's got a point."

Kathryn quickly agreed. "I wonder if they have herbal tea."

"Doubtful, but there's only one way to find out," Lyman said, flipping on the blinker. He pulled the van into the lot, and the four of us piled out. The diner was kinda old, kinda cool, and the bell on the door hadn't finished chiming before the waitress said hello.

The place was busy enough for the breakfast shift, and I figured being on I-84 made it good for locals and travelers alike. Not that the locals looked too happy to see us; a few farming types—coveralls and truckers' caps—turned to stare. I heard a mumble of "damn hippies" and "headed to White Lake" but ignored it. If our choice of clothes and long hair and music wasn't to their liking, they were in for one helluva disappointment because these parts of the State of New York were in for a lesson in counterculture the next three days.

The Aquarian Exposition—3 Days of Peace & Music was rolling into Sullivan County.

We took a booth and ordered. Pauly's mention of eggs and bacon had us all vying for the same, and man, it was good. Life as a college student didn't afford us many luxuries, but then, we weren't big on material things.

"So tell me again," Pauly said after his last forkful. It was like he could only retain information when fed. "Why did Colleen bail?"

I knew Kathryn's reply would be long and I'd heard it all before. I was pretty sure Pauly had too, but he listened intently. "You know she withdrew, right?" she started. "Her parents lined up a secretarial job at their lawyers and insisted she take it. They truly think a woman shouldn't aspire to be anything more than a secretary or a mother…" Kathryn went on. And on. And on.

And then Lyman began on corporate power and privatization and outsourcing and the detriment to the fundamental rights of the people… And so it went on.

I loved Lyman and Kathryn. I really did. They were passionate about our country, total freedom riders, but I'd heard all of this before. More than a few times. And I'd engaged in lengthy debates, but it was a fire in them that would never be contained. Over the years it simply changed direction, rekindled, and on it raged again.

I began to study the other folks in the diner. The hippie-hating farmers were still there, sour-faced, scowling into their cups of joe. And there was a young family; I smiled as the kids enjoyed their pancakes. But then there was a guy, by himself, in a booth staring out the window. He was wearing slacks and a sweater. His blond hair was the good ol' short back and sides. He was so tidy and clean-cut, he couldn't be anything but military. The duffle bag at his feet confirmed my suspicion.

U.S. Army.

Normally I wouldn't look twice at his type, and Lord knew, his type never looked twice at me. But there was a look of such profound sadness on his face, I couldn't look away.

"Gary?" Lyman called my name.

I turned, not having heard any of what he'd said before. The three of them were watching me. "Hey, I'm just gonna go say hi." I took my cup of coffee and slid out of the booth.

"We're leaving in five," Kathryn called after me.

I gave her a nod to let her know I'd heard her and made my way over to the sad army guy. He was still staring out the window, looking like he was fighting tears. "Hey," I said so as not to scare him. I nodded to the seat opposite him. "Can I join you?"

He startled anyway and shifted in his seat. "Oh, sure," he replied.

I slid in and put my coffee between us. "I was just

sitting over there with my friends," I explained. "I couldn't help notice."

His eyes, so blue, shot to mine. "Notice what?"

Wow, okay. So that was an overreaction. And over what? What did he think I noticed? He swallowed hard and looked back out the window, a deep blush staining his cheeks.

I put my hand up. "I couldn't help but notice you were here alone."

He glanced at me again, then kept his eyes on his hands that were now clasped on the table. "Sorry, I… I…" He sighed. "It's been a helluva day."

"It's early morning."

The guy almost smiled, then shook his head. "Feels longer."

It was pretty clear he wasn't having a good day, so I gave him a smile. "My name's Gary Fairchild."

He looked at me then, like really met my eyes. His cheeks pinked up a little. "Nice to meet you, Gary. I'm Richard Ronsman."

CHAPTER TWO

RICHARD RONSMAN

"IT'S BREAKFAST TIME," he said.

Really? This day had gone on so long, it felt like five in the evening. He sat facing me, sliding his coffee across the laminate table. He was a tall guy, thin build, with longish scraggly brown hair and a beard. He wore bell-bottom jeans and a faded purple shirt under a brown corduroy jacket. My dad would call him a good-for-nothing hippie, but he had a smile that pulled at something in my chest.

His eyes were a bluish gray and his lips were pink. His name was Gary, and there was a kindness, an easy peacefulness to him that I envied.

"So, Richard," he said. "What has you sitting alone in this here diner at this time of day? You waiting for someone?"

"Not a someone," I answered with a shake of my head. "The 9:10 bus to New York City."

"I love New York City," he said, still smiling. "What's an army guy going to the Big Apple for?"

I cocked my head. "Army? How did you…?"

"The bag at your feet." He sipped his coffee. "Unless you stole it, but you don't look like the stealing-government-property type of guy."

I almost smiled. "I didn't steal it." I looked at the empty coffee cup and turned it in my hands. "I've finished my time at Fort Polk, Louisiana. I've just been home to see my folks and… and I leave New York for California in a few days."

"What's going on in California?" He seemed genuinely interested. "I always wanted to go."

I swallowed hard. "I'm being deployed to Vietnam," I said, damn near needing to push the words out.

"Oh, man," he replied in a whisper. "I guess that explains why you were staring out the window."

I tried to smile but it didn't feel right.

"Saying goodbye to your folks must've been tough," he furthered. "I can't even imagine."

"Yeah, well, they um…" I let out a long, slow breath. I was just about to divulge too much and stopped myself. "I was going to do some sightseeing in the city. You said you loved it. What's a must-see?"

Gary stared at me for a beat too long. "You know, we're heading to Woodstock. You know, The Aquarian Exposition—3 Days of Peace and Music," he said like he was quoting some ad. "You should totally come with us. We have a spare ticket now because Colleen didn't come. There's enough food and a place to sleep."

"I can't. I'm…"

"You're what?"

"I'm leaving for New York City…"

"Do you have your ticket already?"

"No, I have a military pass…"

"Then you should totally come with us! You said you had a few days. When do you have to be in California?"

"I have to be in New York City for my flight on Monday."

"There will be lines of buses leaving the festival every day. Come along just for one day if you want."

Normally I would have said no, but after the last two days, and considering these would be my last few days on American soil for who knew how long, I actually considered it. But I didn't know this guy or his friends. I glanced over to their table. They looked harmless enough, friendly even, for a bunch of hippies. "I don't know if that's really my scene."

Gary just smiled. "If you're going to war, all the more reason to come. If you're fighting for freedom, for peace, then you gotta see what you're fighting for, right? And I'm pretty sure you don't wanna get all the way over to the other side of the world, trekking through the jungle and being shot at, with any regrets now, do you?"

I stared right at him, into those weird-colored gray eyes. *If only he knew.* I swallowed hard. The truth of his words felt like a gut punch. "Regret is… I um…"

Gary didn't push me to finish. I wasn't even sure I could. "Come with us. If nothing more than for some fresh air and music." His friends made their way to the door and called his name. He gave them a nod, then turned back to me. "Don't leave with any regrets. If you don't wanna come with us, then go to New York City and promise me one thing."

"What's that?"

"That one thing you want, but the one that scares you," he replied. "Do it." He slid out of the booth and stood up. "It was nice to meet you, Richard Ronsman. I hope I made your day a little brighter, like you made mine." He turned, then stopped and faced me once more. "That old blue van with the white stripe?"

I followed his nod to the beat-up Ford Econoline in the lot.

"I'm just going to use the john," he said. "So we'll be leaving in about two minutes, if you wanna join us. No questions asked."

He gave me a smile that made his eyes shine, a gentle dip of his head, and he turned and walked to the restrooms.

Could I? Get into a van with four total strangers and traipse off to some hippie music festival?

I'd always been the responsible one. I always strived for good grades, trying to make my dad happy. Nothing ever seemed to be good enough, not even joining the army was good enough, and Lord knew he would never, ever, approve of me being so irresponsible…

Gary walked out of the restroom and he gave me a frown when he saw I hadn't moved. But he nodded, conceding defeat. "Good luck," he said from across the diner and walked out. The bell at the door chimed with a finality that kicked up my heart rate.

I watched them laughing as they opened the doors to the van, and I knew I had to decide.

Everything was telling me it was such a foolish thing to do. Except my heart. Something told me I had to do this, that I'd regret not joining them.

I grabbed the bag at my feet, threw some money on the table, and raced out the door just as the van door was about to slide shut. "Gary, wait!" I yelled out.

The van door stopped and his smiling face appeared. I threw my bag to him and climbed into the van, smiling for what felt like the first time in weeks, to the strange faces staring back at me. "Um, hi," I said, breathless. I sat next to Gary. His smile was genuine and warm, and I ignored the way my body reacted to him.

Like how I always ignored the way my body reacted to men instead of women.

"Guys," Gary said. "This is Richard. He's coming with us."

CHAPTER THREE

GARY

I DIDN'T MISS the strange look Lyman gave Kathryn in the front seat, and I was pretty sure Richard didn't miss it either. But what I also didn't miss was the smile on Richard's face. It was like he'd freed himself from his cage of responsibility, just for a day or two. It was a sight far removed from the sullen man staring out the window just a few minutes ago.

I made quick introductions, and everyone gave a nod and mumbled hellos as Lyman pulled out of the lot and back onto the road. Kathryn unfolded the map again and was discussing with Lyman which roads to take, and soon enough, we were on our way.

"So, Gary," Pauly said. "You from around here? I mean, I'm guessing you are. Otherwise, what are you doing sitting in the local diner, right?" Pauly nodded to himself. "And that bag ya got there, is that the real army?"

"I promised him no questions," I answered.

"Oh, sorry, man," Pauly said quickly, genuinely apologetic. "'S cool. Man's gotta have his secrets. Mysterious is groovy."

Richard smiled, but he gave a cautionary glance to Kathryn and Lyman in the front. "No, that's okay, I don't mind answering. Yes, I'm from around here. My folks have a farm outside Middletown. And yes, I'm in the army. Well, kind of. I've done my training in Louisiana and I'm flying out for Vietnam in a few days."

Pauly's eyes went wide, Kathryn turned in her seat, and Lyman's eyes went to the rearview mirror.

"That was why I invited him," I replied. "Figured if he was going off to war, he should see what he's fighting for."

That was a logic none of them could argue with.

I knew Kathryn and Lyman's opinions on the Vietnam War, and hell, I tended to agree with them. But political reasons aside, the war itself wasn't Richard's fault.

Pauly leaned back in his seat and stretched his legs out. His long dark hair flopped down over his face and into his long sideburns. "Man, the Vietnam War," he said shaking his head slowly. "That is some heavy shit right there."

I nodded, though Pauly didn't see. He had his eyes closed already. I loved Pauly, I really did. Out of all my friends, he was the most laid back, the most relaxed. He was cool with everything, and his mantra of just letting people be was similar to my own.

"So where are we headed?" Richard asked. He wiped his hands on his thighs and gave me a nervous look.

"A place called White Lake, Bethel," Kathryn said, holding up the map and pointing to the spot she'd marked with a red sticker. "It was supposed to be in Wallkill, but they changed the location."

"Yeah, I remember my dad talking about it," Richard said. Then he leaned forward and pointed to the map. "If you take this road right here, before the lake, and drive north of it, you'll knock a few miles off your trip and maybe beat the traffic."

"Oh, cool. Thanks," she said, then relayed the directions on the map to Lyman.

Richard sat back and we were pretty much touching from our knees to our shoulders. "Sorry," he said quietly. "Not much room."

I turned my head toward him. "I don't mind."

He didn't reply. He just smiled, but there was a flash of something in his eyes, and the blush that pooled in blotchy patterns down his cheek and neck was answer enough.

I was pretty sure Richard didn't mind the body contact either.

THE TRAFFIC WAS LINED up for miles, but we were all too excited to care. We'd heard rumors that people were arriving early, and they weren't wrong. The festival didn't officially start until tomorrow, but we thought we'd get in early and grab a good spot. The place was already packed; the parking lot was nearly full and the huge sweeping field before the stage—which was still being set up—was just a sea of people and blankets and tents.

Every single face I saw was smiling or laughing. A few people were already smoking weed, much to Pauly's happiness. "Right on, man," he said, giving them the peace sign as we walked past, which they all returned. I had no doubt Pauly would be hanging out with them real soon.

But Richard's face was perfect. His eyes were as wide as his smile as he took in the crowds, the scenery, people lying all over the blankets and laughing. It was pretty clear to me that he hadn't seen anything close to this.

For me, it was just like open-air movie nights at our college, just on a much grander scale.

But there was a hum of anticipation here that had me excited too.

"Here's a good spot," I said when we found a bit of a clearing in the crowd. We laid the blanket out and dumped our bags. I had a rolled-up tent, which we could put up later, but first, we ate some lunch, and not long after that, Kathryn and Lyman went back to the van for a while and Pauly wandered off to make new friends. Weed-smoking friends, no doubt.

Richard and I were left sitting on the blanket, legs stretched out, and leaning on our hands. Richard was still smiling, but he nodded to Pauly. "He seems pretty cool."

"Pauly's cool," I replied. "Nicest guy you'd ever meet."

"You guys all go to the same college?"

I nodded. "Western Connecticut State College. I'm doing business management, my final year. Pauly's in my dorm, but he's a math whiz so we're not in any of the same classes."

"A math whiz? For real?"

I laughed at the look on his face. "Yep. Don't let his appearance fool you." It was true. Pauly wore faded bell-bottoms, shirts with holes in them, and his scraggly hair and long sideburns hardly gave the impression he was the Einstein of the math world. "He's doing mathematical science. Smarter than his professors, apparently. They want him to transfer to MIT, but he's not sure."

"Wow."

"I know." I laughed. "I think he's worried they'll try and curb his ways."

Richard smiled. "He's probably right."

"What about you?" I asked. "I mean, I know I said no questions, and you don't have to answer if you don't want, but what's the Richard Ronsman story?"

He sat up and crossed his legs, a change in posture that

said he wasn't too comfortable in answering, but he did. "I didn't go to college. I mean, I got the grades, but my folks have a farm, so I've been helping my dad since I left school."

"Then why the army?" I pressed. I didn't want to push him, but it was such an odd thing. He was a clean-cut, all-American guy, raised on a farm. He had a job in a primary industry, which gave him every right to stay. And he didn't seem happy about it. I'd known him for just a few hours, but even I could see he was quiet and gentle-natured, soft-spoken. He even had a slight lilt to his voice, a little feminine when he wasn't censoring himself. Going to war just didn't make sense.

"It's a long story," he answered quietly.

"Did you get into trouble with the law?"

He shook his head. "No, nothing like that."

And that was it. He said no more, so I let it drop.

After a moment of silence, I asked, "Have you ever seen anything like this?" I nodded toward the crowd.

"Never," he replied; his smile returned. "And people are still lining up to get in."

"The bands start tomorrow. It's gonna be awesome!"

As it turned out, he'd only heard of a few of the names that were advertised. His parents didn't much care for that kind of music, and the more he spoke of his life, his farm, his parents, there was a sadness that lurked in his eyes. It wasn't just sadness from leaving his folks; it was something else. I didn't know what, exactly, but I got a clearer picture of who he was.

And that was a sheltered guy, who'd spent his life on his family farm, never allowed to venture too far from it, but now he was shipping out to fight a war in a foreign country.

If he were a jigsaw puzzle, there were still a lot of

pieces missing. And much to my own surprise, they were pieces I wouldn't have minded searching for.

I nudged his shoulder. "Come on, let's find the toilets."

"They're over that way," a girl on the blanket next to ours said.

"Oh, thanks!" I replied with a smile and a wave, and Richard and I wandered through a sea of blankets and people in the direction she pointed. There were people lying down, some with books, some asleep, some making out. One couple was getting pretty hot and heavy, and Richard's face was hilarious. "Are they just going to do that in front of everyone?" he whispered when we'd walked past.

"Sure, why not?" I replied with a shrug. "Free love and all that."

Jeez. He was acting like he'd never seen people kiss before. I stopped walking to look at him. "Have you ever made out with someone before?"

"Oh, sure," he answered, far too quickly.

I raised my eyebrows at him and he looked away. "It's nothing to be embarrassed about," I said. "Lots of folks haven't, and that's okay."

We began walking again. "I kissed Moira Frankston once," he said after a while. He made a face like the mention of it brought with it a bad memory.

"It wasn't good?" I asked.

He didn't answer, and by then we'd rounded a line of trees to the banks of portable toilets. They were clean enough now, but I'd imagine after three days, they wouldn't be too great. I let Richard go before me, and when I was finished, I found him standing a ways off, waiting. He was turned, looking at someone or something. "Hey."

He spun quickly, and his face was a little pale but

flushed. I'd startled him, obviously, but his face told me something else… I glanced over to where he was looking before and saw what could only be the reason for the expression on his face.

Oh.

It was two guys. They were sitting on their blanket, leaning in and kissing.

And Richard's reaction could mean one of two things. He was horrified and disgusted, or he was astounded, in a good way, and there was a reason his kiss with Moira Frankston hadn't appealed to him.

And his closeness to me in the van, the blush on his cheeks, that look in his eye back in the diner… it all kinda clicked into place. One more piece of the Richard Ronsman puzzle.

"It's just two people in love," I said, still looking at the two guys. "Does it bother you?"

He shot me a look that was more scared than I expected. And I could see it, that split moment where he was about to deny everything, but he searched my eyes for the longest moment before he looked away. "I've just never seen…"

I put my hand on his shoulder, making him jump and meet my eyes again. "It's okay, Richard. Lots of folks haven't, and that's fine. The law doesn't like it much, but there isn't anything wrong with it." I held his gaze. "No matter what they say on television or in church. It's just a couple, like any other, who want to kiss and hold hands."

He looked back at the kissing couple, and I swear it was like he was seeing his own truth for the very first time.

"You okay?" I asked quietly.

He nodded quickly and looked away, taking in a shaky breath and finding some fortitude. "And no one here cares that they're… together like that?"

"Some people do, just like how some folks still get bothered when they see people of different races together." If he'd lived a kinda sheltered life on a farm in a small community, I could only guess his experience with same-sex anything had been sheltered too. "But it doesn't matter what other people think. If it's what you feel in here"—I put my hand to my chest—"it's what you truly feel, then there's nothing wrong with that. It's just love, Richard. What difference does it matter if it's with a guy or a girl?"

His eyes swam, and he swallowed hard as he glanced back at the couple who were now laughing at something. "They look happy," he whispered.

I watched them for a long moment. "They do. Doesn't everyone deserve happiness?"

His gaze shot to mine again, his eyes filled with uncertainty. "Should we head back?"

I smiled at him. "Sure."

CHAPTER FOUR

RICHARD

NEVER IN MY life had I ever seen two men kissing.

I'd dreamed of it. Fantasized about it. Wished for it.

It made my insides curl in a way I never imagined. I felt weak all over, hot and cold at the same time. And aroused and alive. And scared.

And Gary just smiled, and he called it love. He said everyone deserved happiness.

That's not what my dad said.

We got back to our blanket and sat back down. I felt restless and confused, and there were so many people. There were random bursts of singing and guitars and laughter, and it was all a bit much.

"You're overwhelmed," Gary said softly. He drew his legs up to sit cross-legged, and his knee rested on my hip. He was so close, and it should have sent me reeling backward. I glanced around to see if people noticed, but no one had.

Not one person around us looked at us, or cared.

"Richard, I'm gonna tell you something," he said. "Gimme your hands."

I hesitated and looked around us again. No one was paying us a lick of attention at all. I held out my hands and his were warm and strong, and I felt something inside me shift. Like something had been missing for so long and was suddenly found.

"There's nothing wrong with you," he whispered. His face, his perfect face, so serious but gentle and kind. His smile was everything I needed. "There's nothing broken. You're not sick in the head. You don't need fixing. You're not going to hell."

My eyes burned and I couldn't swallow.

"You are perfect just as God made you, just as you are."

I shook my head, but Gary nodded and squeezed my hands. I didn't want to cry, not here, not in front of him. "It's…" What could I say? It was a million different things, and to not deny it meant owning up to it, and I wasn't even sure I could do that. I'd been denying it for so long.

"It's not easy," he said. "Believe me, I know. But it's my truth. And I deserve to be happy."

His truth.

"You… you're…"

He nodded and smiled. "I am. You don't have to say it. It's not an easy word to say because it makes it real. But it gets easier with time. It will get easier for you."

I shook my head. "I'm not…" And I stopped. I couldn't even say it to deny it. Not when he'd been honest with me.

"You're not what?" He said, still smiling. "Happy? Living true to yourself?"

Then there were tears.

I shook my head again, and he let go of one of my hands so he could wipe my cheek. His hand on my face felt so good, I couldn't help but lean into his touch.

"You've been carrying this weight around on your own for so long," he murmured. "You must be so tired."

"I am," I said through more tears. "So tired."

He never told me to stop crying. He never told me to man up. He just wiped my cheeks, and I was suddenly so tired, I could almost fall asleep sitting up. Exhaustion hit me like a ton of bricks.

"Here," he said. "Lie down for a bit." And he coaxed me down, and I couldn't fight it. I had no strength left. I'd never felt this kind of tired. He stretched his legs out, and when I curled onto my side, he put my head on his thigh and I let him.

I closed my eyes, and before I could freak out that I was using his leg as a pillow—a man! I was lying down on another man's leg!—he stroked his fingers through my hair, and with the warmth of the sun on my face, with his strong but gentle touch, I fell asleep.

I WOKE to the sound of singing. It was some folk song I might have heard on the radio, and it took me a second to realize it was the people around me who were singing. There was a warm hand on my arm and a rumbling, deep voice was closer than all the others.

Then I remembered where I was.

I was almost scared to open my eyes. Because if I woke up, this dream would end. This closeness to him would be over, and I'd be forced to face the consequences from before: that I'd admitted my deepest, darkest secret.

But then he said he was too. He was the same as me. How was that even possible?

He'd said it was okay. That nothing was wrong with me, and that I deserved to be happy.

But then the song drew to a close and a round of applause and cheers went up, and then another song began. Someone with a guitar, more voices, and I sat up. Gary was right there, smiling at me as he sung about how many roads must a man walk down, but he was smiling at me as he sang.

The group on the blanket next to ours had the guitar and there must have been fifty people around us singing. Gary moved a little closer to me and he sang a little louder, and it wasn't long until our shoulders were touching and we swayed to the song.

I didn't think I'd ever have the courage to sing, but it was contagious. People the same age as me, around twenty years old, wearing denim jeans and T-shirts, some with daisy chains around their heads or bandanas, men with long hair and floral shirts, vests of fur or fringes. The very kind of people my father would scoff at and call 'no-good hippies.' He'd say they were a burden to society, a smear on the American way of life.

But as I sat with them, sang with them, smiled with them, I had no idea it could feel so good.

I'd never felt freer than I did that very moment.

When that song ended, Gary leaned in and spoke right against my ear. "You okay now?"

I nodded and smiled, genuinely, for the first time since I was a small child. "Thank you. I didn't mean to freak out before."

He put his hand on my back, and it felt like it might burn through the fabric of my shirt. "You're allowed to freak out. It's a lot to take in."

I nodded and found myself smiling at him. But we were a little too close, closer than men should probably be, so to distract myself I checked my watch. It was almost three. "Did I sleep for that long?" I asked him.

"You were out like a light," he replied with a happy smile. "I could stretch my legs a bit though. Wanna take a walk?"

He didn't really wait for an answer. He got to his feet and held out his hand to pull me up, and I gave him my hand without thinking. I let go as soon as I stood up and looked around to see a lot more people had arrived. "Wow."

Gary laughed. "It's a gasser, right?"

I looked at him then. "A gasser?"

"The coolest thing ever," he explained.

"Sorry. I'm not up to date on what the cool kids say." I made a face, but the crowds were staggering. I'd never seen this many people in my life. And I was soon smiling without even realizing.

"This way," Gary said, as he waved me over. We snaked our way through the masses toward the side of the parking lot. It was fenced off and out of the way. There were fewer people there, and the rows of blankets and tents and laughter and song gave way to green grass and quiet. Gary turned to face me, his grin wide, his eyes kind and warm. "Aren't you glad you came with us?"

"I am," I replied. "I'm sorry about before… I never should have…"

"What?" he pressed. "Never should have what?"

"Never should have said what I said. Or admitted to…" I shook my head and let out a shaky breath. "I can't even say it. Does that make me some kind of coward?"

"Coward? Absolutely not. No one has stood in your shoes. Everyone's journey to this point right here is their own, and it ain't up to anyone else to judge how you got here."

I found myself smiling at him. "You have a totally

different way of looking at things than anyone I've ever met." I sighed and leaned against the fence. "I could have done with a friend like you through high school."

"If we had gone to the same high school, do you think we would've been friends?" he asked, still smiling. "Let me guess. You were on the football team."

"Football? I snorted. "Hardly. Baseball."

He laughed. "Well, I wasn't. I was a mathlete and in the drama club. You would've hated me."

"Nah," I said. "I would've envied you."

He stared at me for a long while, then he squinted against the afternoon sun. "If we had gone to school together, maybe I could've tutored you or something after class, and we'd known each other's secret and maybe spend all those hours making out instead of doing homework."

I felt my cheeks heat, and words failed me.

"You ever kissed a guy before?" he asked, still looking at me, squinting one eye from the sun. His beard looked more ginger in the sunlight; his lips looked even pinker. Then the tip of his tongue trailed across his bottom lip, making it shine in its wake.

I swallowed hard and shook my head. The ability to breathe escaped me. "My dad always says people like me are bound for eternity in hell," I blurted out. "'Cept I never told him what I was, but I think he knows. 'Cause he looks at me all mean when he talks about it. Like a threat, ya know?"

Gary frowned but nodded. "You don't actually get to choose who you're attracted to. It's in your makeup, like the color of your eyes. It's just who you are."

"Do you really believe that?"

Gary smiled. "Of course I do. I never made a decision to find Tommy Sutcliffe cute in the third grade. He was crushing on Charmaine Polinski, and I looked at her, then looked at him, and I knew there was no question. I wanted to kiss Tommy, not Charmaine, or any other girl in my class."

I laughed at that. At how ridiculous it was to be having this conversation. Me! Talking about kissing boys instead of girls. "Did you? Kiss Tommy?"

"Nope. My first kiss was Chip Wilding, in the ninth grade."

"Ninth grade?" I couldn't believe it. "Did he… was he…?"

"He kissed me first." He laughed at my expression and leaned back against the fence alongside me. "Guess we had different lives, huh?"

Had or still have? "Do your parents know?"

He nodded and smiled out over the field. "My dad's not too happy about it, being that it's against the law and all, but my mom's fine. We don't talk about it, but they know." He glanced at me, then back out to the crowd of people. "Does your mom know?"

I shook my head quickly. "Oh no. She'd have me exorcized to save my soul from the devil if she knew. Or I'd be living at the church to repent."

"She is aware that priests and ministers are all men, right?" he asked with a wink.

I laughed. "If they're anything like Father Simmonds at my local church, I'd rather not."

Now Gary laughed. "Not good?"

I burst out laughing and made a face. "Even thinking about that is not good."

He pushed off the fence. "Richard, I really like the sound of your laughter. And if you want, no pressure at all, but if you want your first real kiss to be with me, I would be down with that."

My face burned so hot I thought I might catch fire, and I certainly couldn't form a reply. Gary laughed some more and nodded back to the mass of people. "Come on. We better get back."

CHAPTER FIVE

GARY

WHEN WE GOT BACK to our blanket, Kathryn and Lyman were there, and Pauly staggered through the crowd with a goofy smile and slits for eyes. He'd clearly been into someone's stash, but it was impossible not to smile at him. Pauly was the type of guy everyone liked.

We sat for a while, sang some more songs, and Richard never stopped smiling. He didn't know all the words, but he clapped and swayed, a damn sight happier than the man I had seen staring out the window in the diner this morning.

Lyman eyed him cautiously, and I could see Richard was uncomfortable with his scrutiny. It wasn't until we stopped singing so we could eat something that Lyman broke the peace.

"So, Richard," he started, handing him a sandwich. "What's your story?"

Richard's cheeks went pink. He looked to the blanket and then out to the crowd of people. "I had some days to spare," he answered. "Gary asked me if I'd like to come along, and I thought it sounded like a real good idea."

"Some days to spare before what?" Lyman asked. His tone was neutral but his question was pointed enough.

"He's flying from New York City to Los Angeles," I answered for him. They already knew he was going to Vietnam, and I was hesitant to mention it again.

Lyman and Kathryn stared, and I could see their tempers warring with their manners. "The war, huh?" Kathryn asked.

Richard nodded. "Yeah, I did my training in Louisiana, and I came home to see my folks, but..."

"But what?" Lyman asked.

"But my folks and I don't exactly see eye to eye," he replied quietly. His eyes tightened when he looked at Lyman, but he smiled when he looked at me. It wasn't a carefree smile; it was forced and brief at best.

"Do they not agree with the war?" Lyman asked. "Lots of people are opposed to it. You'd be hard pressed to find someone here at this festival who agrees with it."

I shot him a look. "I think he knows that."

Richard gave me a thankful smile. "They're fine with the war. My folks would agree with anything the government says or does. They pray to Jesus and the American flag."

"What about you?" Kathryn asked. "What or whom do you pray to?"

Richard look out across the sea of people and sighed. "Well, I don't know. I've sat in church every Sunday of my life, been to every Sunday school session and every church get-together there was, listening to them preach about how judgment of others is wrong and that forgiveness is good, yet I was surrounded by people who do a whole lot of judging and not a lot of forgiving." Richard's face filled with pain and anger. "And I'd probably believe in Jesus if he believed in me."

Lyman and Kathryn didn't know what to say to that.

I put my hand on Richard's shoulder and rubbed circles on his back. "I'd like to believe there is a God who is free of judgment."

Pauly nodded slowly and lifted his beer. "Amen to that."

We ate in silence for a while, and as the sun began to set, the songs around us died down and tents started to go up. Kathryn and Lyman bid us goodnight and headed back to their van, and although they were still wary of Richard, his little speech on religion painted him in an unexpected light. I didn't think they knew what to make of him.

Pauly was already off talking to different groups of people, so I nudged Richard with my shoulder. "Hope you know how to put up a tent," I said.

"Sure do," he replied with a smile. "Country boy, remember?"

"Got something to say about city boys?" I asked, grinning at him.

"I got plenty," he replied. Then he nudged me with his shoulder and laughed. "Come on, I'll show you how it's done."

He was right about one thing, he knew what he was doing. We pulled the blanket aside and all our gear, and he had that tent up in a flash. We straightened out the blanket on the floor of the tent and threw our bags in just as the last rays of the sun were gone. I rolled out my sleeping bag, pulled out my flashlight from my backpack, and turned it on. "Yeah, okay country boy. You did good."

He laughed and lay down on the blanket, seemingly more at ease now no one else could see us inside the tent. "You didn't do too bad either, city boy." He folded his arms behind his head and stared up at the ceiling. His shirt almost untucked itself and I caught a glimpse of pale skin at his hip. "I suppose I should get used to sleeping on the ground with no sleeping bag. At least I have a tent over me here. God only knows what it'll be like over there."

Over there. He didn't have to say Vietnam. I knew that's where his mind had gone.

"I can do camping for a few days," I allowed. "Though I'll take a running shower and hot water over the great outdoors any day. But I gotta say, the idea of walking into a foreign jungle and sleeping on the ground, not knowing who lurked around, scares the shit out of me."

He nodded. "Me too, if I'm being honest. I always wanted to see the world, but not like this." He rolled onto his side and faced me, one arm tucked under his head for a pillow. "I'm really glad I came here. Thank you for asking me."

The sincerity of his words squeezed my heart. "You're welcome," I replied. "And you can use my flashlight any time if you need to go to the bathroom in the night. And we can unzip my sleeping bag and use it like a blanket, if you like. I only brought one pillow, but we can share that too, if you want."

He sat up and hugged his knees. "You're being very kind."

"No," I replied simply. "Just being human."

He smiled and rested his chin on his knee. "Well, you're one of the kindest humans I've met."

"Kindness is my thing," I said.

"Oh," he laughed. "There I was thinking I was special."

I knew he meant it as a joke, but I could only be honest with him. "You are. I'm not this kind to everyone. I don't share my flashlight with just any stranger I pick up in small-town diners."

He laughed and hid his smile behind his knees. I had so many things I wanted to ask him and, more than that, things I wanted to show him and do to him. Here he was, out in the big gay world for the first time just a few days shy of going off to war…

"I don't think your friends like me too much," he said quietly.

"Lyman and Kathryn? They're okay. They don't like the war, I can tell you that much."

"Oh, well… I don't want to cause trouble between you and your friends." He swallowed hard. "I can be on my way anytime. You just say the word."

"Are you kidding?" I asked. "You're exactly what they need to see."

He shook his head a little and whispered, "And what's that?"

"The human component of war." I took a deep breath and exhaled on a sigh. "They go on crusades about the government all the time. To them, the war is political propaganda, and they think it's the government trying to push some ulterior financial agenda. I mean, Kathryn and Lyman are good people. They're very passionate about, well, everything. Lyman more so than Kathryn. Their latest crusade is government privatization and corporate greed. Last year it was environmental and ecological sustainability and government and corporate greed. And before that, it was women's rights and the government's agenda to moderate women's health because of government and corporate greed."

"I'm beginning to see a pattern."

I laughed. "Oh yeah. They believe the government needs to be watched and held accountable. Which it does, I agree, but Lyman and Kathryn are actively passionate about it. True freedom riders."

He smiled. "And Pauly? What's his crusade?"

"He's just here for the weed."

Now he laughed. "And you? What's your crusade?"

"I believe in the people. I believe in freedom, freedom of choice, freedom of rights." I smiled at him. "I believe in the freedom to fall in love with whoever I want and having my love be equal in the eyes of the law and the church."

He stared at me for a long moment, his eyes becoming glassy. "I like your crusade. That'd be mine too, if I was brave enough."

"You're going to war. I think that makes you brave."

"Or crazy," he mumbled. He shook his head and blinked back his tears. "Wanna know why I signed up?"

I nodded. I mean, I did want to know, but I had a feeling I wouldn't like what he was going to say.

"So my dad would think I was a man," he said. This time, when his eyes filled with tears, one spilled down his cheek. He quickly scrubbed it away. "He looks at me and I can see him thinking that I'm one of those *sissy boys* he rants about. He glares at me, all angry, and tells me those queer men are bound for hell, and he says it like a threat. As if he knows."

Another tear, and another. He tried to wipe them away but they kept on falling.

"So I enlisted," he whispered. "Because then I'd be a man in his eyes. Part of me thinks he won't care too much if I don't come back. If I die in Vietnam, then he can tell all his church friends that I died a hero while secretly being thankful that he's rid of his boy who talks a little too girly for his liking."

"Oh, Richard."

He dried his face and sniffled. It was a resigned sound. "It's okay. I'm used to it. Been dealing with him my whole life."

I took his hand and held it tight in mine. "That doesn't make it right," I said. "You're perfect just as you are, and if your old man can't see that, then he's the one with the problem. It's his loss. Seems to me he's missing out on knowing a pretty great guy."

Richard smiled first, then laughed and shook his head like I was being ridiculous. He looked at our joined hands for the longest moment. "I never thought I'd ever get to hold hands with another man," he murmured. He turned my hand over and threaded our fingers, like he was committing everything to memory. His brow furrowed as if he had more to say but struggled with the words, so I lifted our hands and kissed his knuckles. Then I turned his hand over and kissed the inside of his wrist, and he gasped quietly. "What you said before," he started. His cheeks were flushed, and he licked his lips nervously. "When I saw those two guys kissing… you said…" His words ran out of steam, but he was so nervous and shy, it was almost painful to watch.

I was pretty sure I knew what he was trying to say. "I said if you wanted your first real kiss to be with me, I'd be down with that."

He nodded quickly and let out a rush of breath, followed by a laugh. He ran his free hand through his short hair. "I um…"

"Do you want me to kiss you?"

His eyes flashed to mine, scared and hopeful. Then he nodded again. "Yeah."

I switched the flashlight off so we didn't cast shadows, then took his hand and put his palm to my cheek, letting him feel my beard. I kissed his palm and let him touch his fingertips to my lips. He gasped again, and I ran my thumb over his bottom lip, along his jaw, feeling his stubble there. His eyes were dark and he was breathing hard, and I leaned in, real slow. I held his jaw, and I swear, when our lips touched, I saw fireworks in his eyes.

I kissed him soft and sweet at first, then a little more. Open lips and gentle, and when his eyes closed, I gave him a hint of my tongue. A moan caught in his throat and he deepened the kiss, and I let him. I let him set the pace. I let him take what he wanted, what he needed.

He held my face, his fingers found my hair, and all of a sudden, this kiss became something else. Intensity and heat flared, his tongue in my mouth, and a guttural moan sent a jolt of desire to my groin. Without breaking the kiss, he pushed me back and climbed over my legs so he could straddle me.

Then, as though he realized what he'd just done, he stopped. He put his forehead to mine and squinted his eyes closed. "Sorry, I"

I gripped his hips to keep him right where he was. "Don't apologize," I whispered. "You liked it?"

He barked out a laugh, and when his eyes met mine, there was light and happiness. "Loved it. It feels right. Your beard, and your rough hands, and strong body. That's what it's supposed to feel like for me."

I shifted my hips a little but kept him on top of me. "For someone who's never done much kissing, you're exceptionally good at it."

He blushed and laughed. "I should probably get off you now."

"Or you can stay right where you are and keep kissing me," I said. "We were just getting to the good part."

He made a face. "I've never…"

I sat up a bit and pulled his legs so they wrapped around me. His ass on my cock felt so good, but this had to be about him. "Lucky for you, I have. So how about you go as fast or as slow as you want, whatever you're ready for."

His face burned now and he cringed. "I don't even know where to start. I mean, I've dreamed of it, but I've never…" He swallowed hard. "I've never even seen men kiss until today. Let alone much else."

I cupped his cheeks and waited for him to look me in the eye. "Richard," I murmured. "Would you like me to make you come?"

His eyes widened and he sucked back a breath, but his hips rolled as if he had no say in it. Then he nodded and crushed his mouth back to mine. He held me tighter and squirmed and grinded on me, and I let him for a while. But I soon slowed our pace, and ever so gently, I laid him on his back. His eyes were wide and vulnerability lurked there, with desire and a little fear.

"I'll take care of you," I said, pressing my weight on him. He spread his legs wider and pulled my face to his, bringing our mouths together in a sensual, deep kiss. I rolled my hips and he groaned. I could feel his hard erection, and I had no doubt he could feel mine too.

I was pretty sure if we kept going, I could make him come just like this, but I wanted to make his first time something special. So I kissed down his jaw, down his neck, and I lifted his shirt up so I could kiss his chest, down his stomach, and I looked up to his face to find him leaning up, watching, transfixed by me.

I grinned and popped the button on his pants. "Oh man," he breathed, then fell back onto the sleeping bag.

"I'm going to take you into my mouth," I said. "Is that okay?"

He scoffed. "You keep talking like that and it'll be all over."

I smiled and undid his zipper, then pulled him free of

his briefs. He had a gorgeous cock. Six and a half inches, great girth, and a beautiful head that was made for sucking. I breathed his scent in, drew my nose up the length of his shaft, followed by my tongue. Precome beaded at the slit, and I flattened my tongue to lick it off.

"Oh God," he breathed. His whole body was tense, strung taut. If he was nervous or too close to coming, I wasn't sure. Or maybe he was uncomfortable…

"Richard," I murmured from between his legs, and I waited for him to lift his head and look at me. "Is this what you want? Are you okay with this?"

He let his head fall back with a dull *thunk* and he sighed. "If you stop, I think I might die."

That made me chuckle, and I licked him again for good measure. Then I fisted the base of his cock and took the head into my mouth, and he cried out, his body jerking. His cock pulsed and he fisted my hair. "Oh God. Oh God," he hissed quietly.

I hummed around him, to let him know I was enjoying it as well. Then I sucked a little harder and pumped him, and he let out a harsh groan. "Gary, I'm gonna… I'm gonna…," he rasped.

I groaned and took him deeper, and his back arched, his hips rolled, and his cock pulsed and spilled into my throat. I drank him down and he shuddered and moaned.

I let him go and slid up his body, planting kisses as I went. He had a glazed-over look on his face, his eyes unseeing, and he wore a disbelieving grin. I couldn't help but laugh. "You alive in there?"

He took a second to focus on me. "I've never been more alive."

I lay down on him, keeping my weight on my elbows. I pecked a kiss to his lips. "You're so receptive to touch," I murmured, kissing down his jaw.

He shivered and spread his thighs some more, hooking his foot around my leg. "I can feel your…" He cringed. "You're turned on."

"Of course I am," I said with a smile. "You're hot as hell, and I really like sucking dick. Made me horny."

"Oh." He blanched.

"Talking about sex and dicks and hard-ons is new to you, isn't it?"

He nodded.

"But don't worry, I don't expect you to reciprocate. This was all for you," I said. I kissed under his ear and took his lobe in between my lips. He gasped and ran his hand over my ass.

"I want to," he said. "I want to do to you… what you did to me."

I pulled back so I could look into his eyes. "You don't have to."

"I want to. I probably won't be any good at it," he said with a cringe. "But I'd really like to try."

I kissed his lips again. "Okay." I rolled us over so he was on top of me. "Don't try and take in too much, and don't swallow."

"Why?" he looked at me with all his wide-eyed, country-boy charm. "Don't you like it?"

I barked out a laugh. "Oh, I like it very much. I just don't want you to do anything you're not ready for."

"I want to do it," he replied quickly. He licked his lips. "Will you teach me how?"

I put my hand to his face. "Okay."

He smiled, and he really was very handsome. There was something sweet and earthy about him that appealed to me. He was naïve to the world and so very opposite of all the guys I knew at college. "We sometimes forget the rest of our bodies when it comes to sex. But touch and intimacy is a whole-body experience, not just with our dicks."

He blushed and swallowed hard. "What do I do first?"

"Kiss me, slow and deep," I whispered. "Then explore my neck and chest. Learn how to please all of me."

He crushed his mouth to mine, so I spread my legs for him and he replied with a roll of his hips. I slid my hands under his shirt, over the skin of his back, and he deepened the kiss. When he pulled back, he smiled and laughed like a kid on Christmas morning. He shuffled down a bit and pulled at my shirt, then ran his fingers through the hair on my chest. I was by no means hairy, but he sighed. "You have no idea how good that feels," he whispered, then he leaned down and kissed my breastbone, then he tongued my nipples, making me moan.

"You like that?" he asked.

"Love it."

That spurred him on, and he was all wet mouth and roaming hands and hot breath, and for a novice, he sure knew how to press my buttons.

But the ache in my balls was begging for release and grinding, searching for more friction, and I wasn't getting enough. "Undo my jeans," I urged him. "I need more."

He knelt back on his haunches and took his time popping the button. He licked his lips as he undid the fly, and holy hell, his excitement, his nervousness was driving me closer and closer to the edge.

He pulled the front of my briefs down and gasped quietly when he touched my cock.

"You like it?" I asked.

He nodded, and finding some courage, he freed my cock and ran his hand over the length. "I never thought I'd ever…," he whispered.

"Stroke me," I said. He did, and I thrust into his hand. "That feels amazing."

He leaned in close, inhaled deeply, and his hot breath on the exhale felt so good. He pumped me, watching the skin slide under his touch, like he couldn't believe his eyes. Then he licked the head, softly at first, then again a little harder. He flattened his tongue and tasted precome, and he closed his eyes and moaned.

Then, just like I wanted him to, he closed his lips around the head and took me into his mouth. He was slow and tentative, and there was something perfect about that. It was new and everything he'd only ever dreamed of, and he was savoring every moment, every touch, every taste.

I ran my fingers through his hair and he glanced up at me, his still innocent eyes despite my cock in his mouth. "Oh fuck, yes," I murmured. "So good, Richard. So good."

It took all of my willpower not to thrust, not to fist his hair and fuck his throat. I wanted to come so bad…

He worked my cock a little harder, a little deeper, and his cheeks were flushed pink and his lips were red and wet, gliding over me like silk.

"I'm close," I said, giving him a warning.

A look of determination flashed in his eyes, and he sucked harder, pumped the base of my shaft like I'd done to him. I'd expected him to pull off, to chicken out, but he wanted it.

So I gave it to him.

I let go of my restraint and my orgasm washed over me, through me. I groaned with the force of it.

He made a noise of distaste and I remembered the surprise of it my first time. I couldn't help but chuckle at the look on his face. But, he shocked me again by swallowing. I laughed then and pulled him up into my arms, rolling us onto our sides, and he was quick to bury his face into my chest.

I let the silence sit for a while, giving him time to get his head around what we'd just done. "How are you feeling?"

"Um, great," he murmured.

"Not freaked out at all?"

He pulled back and looked me in the eye. "Should I be?"

I traced a line from his eyebrow down to his jaw. "Not at all. I'm just checking you're okay. It was your first time with a guy, and that can be a little daunting."

He studied my eyes for a long time. Then he said, "Gary, I want to do it all."

"What do you mean? Do what all?"

"Everything. I have two days left before I need to leave for New York, and I might never get the chance again. Even if I come back from Vietnam… I'll never get to be me again. Like I am here with you."

I cupped his face. "What did you want to do?"

"Everything," he said with a grin. "Everything my dad and his preacher friends would hate. Drinking, dancing. And… and… I want you to… I don't want to go to Vietnam a virgin."

"Technically, what we just did was sex." I kissed him softly and whispered, "You're no longer a virgin, Richard."

"No, I mean… I want you to have me…" He squeezed his eyes shut and ducked his head. "I don't know how to ask for it. It's so embarrassing."

I lifted his chin and kissed him again. "Don't ever be embarrassed to ask for something." His cheeks were so red I could feel the heat of them on my palm. "Do you want me to fuck you? Anal sex, is that what you want?"

He cringed, but then he nodded and tried to look away. "When I dream of it, when I fantasize, that's what I want.

Is that wrong? Should I even want that? Doesn't that make me the fruity one?"

I pulled his chin back and waited for him to meet my eyes. "It's not wrong, and you're not fruity. I hate that term. Sex is a beautiful thing. And yes, if it's what you want, that's perfectly fine. And normal. Don't think you're not equal by wanting to receive, okay? It doesn't make you any less of a man."

"Am I that obvious?" he shook his head and scoffed.

"No. But I can guess if your dad preaches that homosexual men are evil, then being the one who catches is the worst kind."

"Catches?"

"Yeah, the guy who catches, like in baseball; there's the guy who pitches and the guy who catches, if you know what I mean. The guy who receives."

"Oh." He chuckled and sighed. "There's so much I don't know. You must think I'm pretty uncool."

"I actually think you're kinda great."

His eyes widened. "You do?"

"Hell, yes. I didn't know clean-cut, all-American boys were my thing, but apparently they are. Well, you are."

He blushed again and buried his face against my chest, seemingly lost for words. So I rubbed his back for a while, just enjoying the closeness, then kissed the side of his head. "So let me get this straight. You want to spend the next two days, before Uncle Sam slaps a uniform on you, having all the sex, drugs, and rock 'n' roll your body can take?"

"Anything and everything that would make my dad flip out."

I laughed. "I'm sure I can help with that."

CHAPTER SIX

RICHARD

I WANTED TO EXPERIENCE EVERYTHING. And when I said everything. I meant it, in every sense of the word. I'd only ever had a sip or two of beer before. My dad always said that alcohol was a curse and it gave men impure thoughts. It made them reckless and ungodly. And dancing with girls was supposed to be supervised in our church group, and my God, never with a man. But as the night grew late, after we'd lain in the tent talking for a while—and we made out some more—impromptu music and singing broke out in the mass of people, and Gary wanted me to experience it.

We made ourselves presentable and he took my hand and led me out into the dark. Some campfires spotted the night, others had lamps, and it was surprisingly light under the moon. A bit of a crowd had gathered around one camp where they were playing guitars and singing, and people were drinking and dancing. Everyone was so happy and welcoming. People my parents would have frowned upon, looked down at: men with long hair and sideburns, open shirts, and flared pants. Women with their hair down, in peasant shirts and long skirts. They all wore necklaces with peace signs, and I'd have thought it was cliché if I wasn't seeing it for myself.

This wasn't dress-up or a costume party like I'd seen on the television. This was the real deal. These were people who believed in the message of peace and freedom.

There was even a man with long, wild hair who was bare-chested but wearing a long skirt. He was dancing surrounded by people yet by himself, with his eyes closed, swaying with his hands up. I'd never seen anything like him, and I couldn't look away.

"Does that shock you?" Gary stood behind me, his lips at my ear.

I shook my head, transfixed by the dancing man. "I've never seen anyone so free."

Gary laughed and put one arm around my waist. He started to move to the music. "Come on, dance," he murmured.

I shook my head. "I… I can't."

He didn't insist, but he kept his rhythm, slowly swaying to the music behind me. Pauly found us, and he floated toward us, clearly stoned, and a beer in each hand. "Heyyyyy," he said, his eyes barely open slits.

"Hey, man," Gary replied, his voice warm at my ear.

"Hey," I said, not sure if I should or not. I edged away from Gary, not wanting to be seen with another man. Which was ridiculous. We were surrounded by people. But still… I wasn't ready for public displays no matter how much I wished for it.

Gary tightened his arm around me and pulled me against him, my back to his front. "I got you," he murmured. "No one's looking, no one cares. Take a look around us."

I risked a glance at the people closest and found no one

staring in disgust. No one ogling or mocking, scornful. No one screaming bible verses or spitting at us.

No. Just other people singing and dancing and being themselves. Other couples, man and woman, and over on the other side was a couple, two women: one with braids and one with short hair, dancing and kissing.

I relaxed into Gary's hold and realized then he had one of Pauly's beers. "Here, have some," Gary said, handing me the can.

I took a mouthful. It was kinda warm and not great, but I drank it anyway. Gary had one hand on my hip, the other around my chest, and he rested his chin on my shoulder as he laughed at something Pauly said. Gary was so relaxed, so confident, it was hard not to admire that.

He was everything I wanted to be.

He was free to be himself.

And that was something I could never be.

I offered the beer back to Gary but he nudged his nose just behind my ear. "You have it."

So I did. Which was probably why, twenty minutes later, I had a buzz going on and was leaning back into Gary.

The atmosphere was contagious. People sang and danced, clapped and laughed. So I did too.

Not as freely as most everyone else, but even the fact I swayed and sang was a milestone. The fact I stood, leaning against a man with his arm around me, a man who I'd just gotten to third base with.

I couldn't ever remember being this happy.

But when Gary suggested it was time for bed, I eagerly agreed. Except Pauly came with us, and as soon as he was in the tent, he crashed out on the floor beside Gary's sleeping bag and was snoring before I could close the tent flap.

Gary pulled me down onto his makeshift bed and was quick to embrace me. "I wasn't expecting company," I admitted. "I was hoping we could… you know…"

Gary held my chin and kissed me. It was a long and lazy kiss, and it was amazing. "We have time for that," he whispered when we broke for air. "This is kinda boss too, though."

"Boss?"

He laughed. "It's cool. Hip. Gas. Mint. Out of sight. The very best."

And he was right.

Lying in each other's arms and kissing, feeling his beard, feeling his strong hands, his hard body, was all of those things.

WAKING up in the arms of a man was like a dream come true. I lay there, as the sun broke the dawn, not wanting to ever move. Outside our tent was already a hive of activity, and I couldn't wait to see what the day would bring.

But right there, lying on the tent floor with Gary's arm wrapped tight around me and my back to his front… Well, I didn't want to ever move.

I could feel his chest, his stomach, his cock against my ass… his thighs even pressed to the backs of mine. I think they called it spooning, and it was incredible. I never thought such intimacy was possible. I didn't think men did this kind of thing with other men. God, I was so naïve. I never thought for one second I could have this. And after this weekend, when I left this craziness behind, I knew I'd never have it again.

I stored every moment in my memory. Every inch of his body, every breath. And even though I could feel his hard cock against my ass, as much as it excited me and thrilled me, just being in his arms was somehow the best thing.

I wasn't lying when I told Gary I wanted to experience it all, and I couldn't wait for the day to begin, but I also wanted to stop time forever.

"Man, I need to piss."

Pauly's voice startled me. I'd forgotten he was in the tent with us. But Pauly sat up, scrubbed his hands over his face, and scooted over to the zippered door. The sound of the zip and then outside voices roused Gary, and he froze for a moment, like he wasn't sure who he had his arm around. But then he sighed, tightened his hold on me again, mumbled my name, and nuzzled the back of my head.

"Morning," I said.

"Hmm."

"I have to say, I've had some pretty good mornings, waking up. Like Christmas or my birthday. But this is, without a doubt, my favorite so far."

Gary chuckled. "When is it?"

"Christmas? Uh, December twenty-fifth."

Gary laughed, his whole body shaking. "No, silly. Your birthday."

"August twenty-seventh."

"That's soon. Like ten days away."

"Yep. I'll be in Vietnam," I said quietly. "Never had a birthday away from home before. Not a Christmas either."

Gary sighed and gave me a squeeze. He didn't say anything for a while, but eventually he said, "And that reminds me. We've got an agenda for you today." He sat up and I lay flat on my back, missing his warmth, his touch already.

"Agenda?" I asked. "To do what?"

Gary looked back at me and smiled. "Everything."

AND WELL, everything started with a walk to the bathroom, something to eat, and brushing our teeth before heading back to our tent to pull it down so the folks behind us could see. The crowd had grown again since last night, and there were literally thousands of people. Tens and tens of thousands of people. No, hundreds of thousands. I'd never seen so many people in my entire life.

And they were still coming.

So many people were trying to make their way in, that the roads were gridlocked so bad that the singers and bands couldn't get in. So people in the crowd with guitars would play and others would sing, and it was the most amazing thing. Everyone was happy and peaceful, and these people—who my parents despised—were what I'd been missing my whole life.

We ate the last of our breakfast, and it wasn't long after that the festival was announced and the first band played. People cheered, sang, and danced; a standing ovation to every song. And it wasn't long after that I was offered a beer and Pauly lit a joint and handed it to me.

I balked at first, but Gary gave me a nudge. "Try everything, remember?"

So I did. I tried it all. I drank more beer, I smoked more weed. Then I danced and sang, and Gary put his arms around me, and right there in front of everyone, I kissed him.

No one cared.

No one that I saw, anyway.

And hours later, the festival was in full swing and we were still dancing and singing when thunder rolled overhead. So we quickly put up the tent and zipped the festival on the outside, leaving just me and Gary inside.

He pulled me close and we kissed, lying on each other and grinding, with desperate hands and eager bodies. When more storm clouds rumbled overhead, he cupped the side of my face, his eyes dark and honest. "Do you still want to experience everything?"

I knew what he was asking. Did I want to have sex? I nodded. "Yes."

My nerves ratcheted up a notch and I was suddenly a little overwhelmed.

"Hey." He brushed his thumb over my cheek. "You don't have to."

"No. I want to. I want this. And I want it to be you."

He smiled. "I promise I'll go slow. I won't hurt you. I'll make love to you so tender you'll never want it to end."

Warmth bloomed in my belly, and my heart squeezed at his words. "Oh God."

Then as the rain began to fall and the music still played outside, I let him have my body, in ways I never knew I could. At first, I thought it was too much. It hurt a little and the stretch and intrusion felt wrong, but he was so tender, so loving, that I soon relaxed and even began to enjoy it.

I gave that part of myself to him, and he was gentle and strong, caring and considerate. Everything he did was for me. And when he moved inside me, sliding and pushing, filling me with his cock and kissing me so sweet, I knew —I just knew—I'd given him my heart as well.

CHAPTER SEVEN

GARY

MAKING love to Richard was different. Sure, I'd been with guys before, but there was something special about him. Maybe being his first made it different, but the way he looked at me, the way he responded to me, it did something crazy to my heart.

When we were done, I made sure he was okay. I pulled the sleeping bag over us and, facing him, held his hand. "How do you feel?"

"Good," he answered. "I mean, fine. A little sore maybe, but not as bad as what I was thinking it might be."

I brought his hand up to my lips and kissed his knuckles. "And apart from the physical difference?"

He chuckled and ducked his head a bit. "I feel like… I feel like *me*. Like the *real* me, for the first time ever." His gaze shot to mine, and even in the darkness I could see the seriousness in them. "I don't know if I'll ever be able to thank you."

"Thank me?"

"For giving me this. I might not ever have this again."

"Yes, you will," I answered. "I'm certain of it."

"How can you know that?" he asked quietly. "I might not even come back from Vietnam."

I pulled him in close. "Don't say that. You'll be fine. You'll come back, and you can live your true life. The life you want, not the life you feel obligated to live."

He snuggled into my chest. "You sound so sure."

I pulled the sleeping bag up and settled in, kissing his forehead. "I am sure."

THE NEXT DAY, it rained. And then it rained some more, and the field that had been lush grass was soon a mudslide. Yet everyone was happy, and the only word I could use to describe it was peaceful. We danced, laughed, talked, met new friends. Richard hadn't stopped smiling yet.

Even though the weather was terrible and no bands could take the stage, spirits were high, kindness and generosity were everywhere.

So were alcohol and drugs. I wasn't strictly opposed to taking drugs; I'd done my share at college parties. And Richard had smoked some weed the day before, but when the group Pauly had befriended offered Richard a tiny square of parchment paper doused with LSD, I intervened.

"Maybe half," I suggested. "They can be pretty strong."

Richard looked up at me. "Should I?"

"If you want to try everything...," I said. "I'll stay sober and look after you. But only take a half."

He nodded and did as I suggested. And half an hour later, it hit him. Creedence Clearwater Revival, Janis Joplin, and The Who played, hundreds of thousands of people began to sing and dance and cheer, and Richard stood there, dancing in slow motion. His arms were raised, his eyes closed, and he swayed. He was completely free. All his inhibitions were gone.

He had stubble now, blond like his hair, his clothes were muddy and wet like the rest of us, and he was the most handsome guy I'd ever seen.

Lyman nudged me with his elbow. I hadn't noticed him and he was quick to smile. "Soldier boy's caught your eye," he said. Lyman and Kathryn knew I liked men, so it was no surprise.

I kept watching Richard, like I said I would. He was high as a kite and I was thankful he'd only had a half. "He's… not like anyone I've ever met."

"He's a cog in the war machine," he started. There was no malice in his tone, but I didn't care for what he was saying.

"He's not. His reasons aren't what you think."

"So innocent people need to die because he has reasons?"

I sighed. "That's not fair."

"The government agenda—"

"Spare me the lecture, Ly." He hated being called that. "You know my views on the war and the government. But Richard's not like them."

"He'll have a gun in his hand soon enough and—"

"Gary," Richard called. He had a goofy smile and glassy eyes. He held his hands out, palms up, and looked up at the sky. "The rain will wet the rabbits."

I snorted. "Rabbits?"

He grinned. "They're so fluffy."

I laughed, and as the rain began to fall, I considered telling him to stop dancing, but he took his shirt off and raised it to the sky. His eyes were closed, and he danced some swaying prayer to the rain gods, and I'd never seen anything so beautiful.

"Dance with me," he said.

So I did. I took off my shirt too, left in only jeans, and for as long as the rain fell, we danced.

BY THE TIME the sun was going down, the entire field was a quagmire. People were lying in the mud, sliding, laughing. The conditions were horrendous, yet no one argued, no one fought. But with the state of us, there was no way we could try to sleep. We were soaking wet, covered in mud, and Richard was still a little high. So, like a few hundred other people, he thought stripping off and skinny-dipping in the farmer's pond was the logical thing to do.

And because of the rain delays, the bands played well past midnight. The darkness was lit by the stage and lanterns burned sporadically, and from where we were on the top of the hill, it looked like a sea lit by fireflies and the warm glow made Richard look like an angel.

"Have you ever seen anything so beautiful?" he asked.

I shook my head slowly, not taking my eyes off him. "No."

"I'm starting to feel not so good," he said, still smiling. I'd wondered when he would come down.

"Here," Pauly said, having heard him. "Have a toke of this."

Without questioning, without hesitation, Richard took the pipe and inahled deeply. He kind of coughed a little bit, but then he laughed and handed it to me. "Come on, Gary," he said. "Join in the fun."

I took the pipe and gave Pauly a glance. "Do I wanna know what's in this?"

Pauly just laughed and said, "Idealism and the intangible vanguard of the new revolution."

Richard stared at him, slow blinked, then roared with laughter. Laughing too, I drew back on the pipe. Then we danced and sang and took pills around breakfast time so we could dance and sing some more.

And around mid-morning on Sunday, when there was a break in the rain, the humidity ratcheted up, and Richard came down.

"You're exhausted," I said. "I could sleep for a bit, if you want me to put the tent up. Out of the way of the people."

He put his hand to his head like he had to hold it up. "I don't want to miss a thing."

"A few hours is all," I suggested.

"Gary, I gotta get to New York City." He scanned the massive crowd. "Somehow."

"Today?"

"This afternoon. This evening at the latest, if I can find a bus that'll get me there by morning."

My stomach fell to my feet. "I'm not ready to say goodbye to you."

He stared at me, his tired eyes and a slow but sad smile. "Me either. I can't tell you how much this means to me. What it has meant to me to be here, to see this. To meet you. I never knew I could… I never thought I'd ever find…" He licked his lips and looked away.

I stepped in closer and whispered so only he could hear. "This isn't the end of us," I said. "No way, no how."

"How can it not be?" he asked, shaking his head. His eyes were glassy again, this time from tears.

"We'll write when you're away," I replied. "And when you get back, you'll find me, or I'll find you. And we'll meet again, just you wait and see."

His bottom lip trembled. "What if I… what if I don't make it back?"

"No," I said, pulling him into my arms, not caring who saw or who might take issue with it. This, *he*, was more important. "Don't even think it. You'll be better than fine. And when you get back, we'll get to do this right."

He held onto me tight and pressed the side of his head to my chest. "I think we kind of did it just right this time."

I rubbed his back. "Me too."

"I'm tired, Gary."

"Me too."

"Can we sleep a bit?"

"'Course we can."

"I wish we had one more night," he murmured.

"Come on, let's go set the tent up. Somewhere out of the way."

He nodded, snuffling his head on my chest. "Yes, please."

We took the tent and our bags and moved to the fringes the best we could. It was muddy everywhere, and the road in was nothing but a parking lot; seemingly endless jagged lines of cars and vans parked at all angles. "Do you think anyone would mind if we set up camp between the cars?" Richard asked.

I snorted. "There are four hundred thousand people here who've shared everything from water to beds, food and clothes. No one will mind at all."

It was a stroke of genius, really. We found a gridlock of parked cars and pitched the tent on the embankment side. It was on a bit of a slant but it was private enough, and we'd no sooner crawled in, laid down, than Richard put his head on my chest, and he was asleep.

I tightened my arm around him and closed my eyes.

The sound of music, laughter, singing, and constant chatter became white noise, and the lack of sleep and use of drugs had sleep dragging me under.

THE SOUND of a bullhorn and laughter close by woke us up, and Richard jolted away from me, startled and frightened, no doubt, that he'd be caught lying with a man. "Hey," I crooned. "It's okay. No one can see us inside the tent."

He let out a breath and sagged but lay back down, his head on my chest. "Do you know what time it is?"

I checked my watch. "Just after three."

"I'll have to go soon."

"I don't want you to."

He let out a shaky breath. "I don't want to go. Four days ago, I was glad to be going. I'd had all the lectures from my father that I could stand, and in a way, I kind of agreed with him. That maybe if I didn't come back from Vietnam, it'd be a blessing. I didn't want to live a lie but couldn't ever be myself either. It was killing me inside," he whispered. I gave him a squeeze and let him get all this off his chest. "And my dad was adamant that I'd come back when my tour of duty was done, and I'd find a girl and settle down. That's what real men did, he said. They got married and didn't shame their parents. None of that sissying around like those hell-bound homosexuals." He imitated a voice I assumed was his father's.

"Oh, Richard," I murmured. "You know that's not true. We're not bound for hell any more than anyone else. I bet your dad preaches the commandment *thou shall not judge*, yet he does an awful amount of judging of others." I tapped his arm. "Look at me, Richard," I whispered, and I waited till he propped his head up and met my gaze. "You not coming back from war is not a blessing, you hear me? You have to come back. We've got unfinished business, you and me."

He almost smiled. "What do you mean, unfinished business?"

"Well, a real first date for starters. Where I buy you dinner and maybe we see a movie. A real cliché burger joint, then maybe a drive-in."

He smiled more genuinely now.

"And a second date, and a third. And by then I'm hoping we'd get past third base."

He barked out a laugh. "I think we're well past that."

"But I'd do it right. In a bed, in a bedroom, with the lights down low and music playing."

"Well, we had a flashlight and some band called Arlo Guthrie."

Now it was me who laughed. "And we can go hiking on weekends, and you can cook me dinner when I'm studying, then I'll cook when you work, and then you can distract me from studying in all the ways you can think of."

He sighed happily and put his head back to my chest. "You make it sound like a fairy tale."

"It can be a reality if you want," I said. "You just need to come back from Vietnam, okay?"

He hummed. "Well, now I have a reason to."

"How long will you be gone for?" I asked.

"Twelve months. And I don't know where they'll send me after that. I signed up for four years."

I frowned. "That's such a long time."

"Having second thoughts already," he said, trying for a joke, but there was a question in his tone.

"Not at all," I answered. "We'll get through Vietnam first, then deal with the rest later. You'll be away for your birthday and Christmas, so we'll have to make up for it next year."

He whispered, "If only I'd met you before I decided to join."

"I know. But I mean it. We'll stay in touch, okay?"

He was quiet, staring at the side of the tent. "I don't regret anything we did, I want you to know that. I actually want to thank you for asking me to come here with you. I wasn't going to. I mean, it was ridiculous for me to get in a van with four complete strangers and go to a music festival, but I've had, without a doubt, the best weekend of my life. I've known you for a handful of days, but you know me better than anyone else in my life."

"Well, just so you know, I don't normally walk up to strangers in diners and ask them to come with me. But as soon as I saw you, something in my bones told me to go to you."

"I'm so glad you did. I had no idea, Gary," he whispered. "No idea that this was even possible for a guy like me."

"You said you wanted to do everything," I murmured. "Anything else you want to do before you go?"

"If last week someone had told me that I'd meet a guy, a hippie no less, and I'd lose my virginity, take drugs, dance in the rain, and swim naked in front of thousands of people, I would've thought they'd gone and lost their mind." I sighed again. "And we could've spent my last few hours here doing all sorts of ungodly things, but I can honestly say, just lying here with you like this, me listening to your heart and your arm around my shoulder, well that's kind of perfect too… Or what did you call it? A gasser."

Chuckling, I gave him a squeeze. "It is. Though we could give you a goodbye with a certain happy ending, if you know what I mean. Something for you to remember when you're in some jungle over there and need some happy thoughts to get you through."

He bit his bottom lip. "What do you have in mind?"

"Well, I'd really like to feel you in my hand and watch your face when you come."

He scoffed out a laugh and his face burned. "You can't just say stuff like that to me!"

I laughed. "But you want me to do it, right?"

He glanced at me, then looked away like he was too embarrassed. But he nodded real quick. "Yes."

"Then kiss me."

His breath caught and he stared at my mouth and leaned up and crushed his lips to mine. It was a hard and desperate kiss, full of all his emotions. I could taste them on his tongue.

I found his jeans fly and popped the button, and his kiss faltered. When I slid my hand into his briefs and took hold of his cock, he shuddered and I smiled against his mouth.

"You're so hard," I whispered.

He moaned, like it was all he was capable of.

"Do you want to touch me?" I asked.

He nodded and ducked his head to my shoulder. I rolled us onto our sides, facing each other, and he could use my arm as a pillow.

He fumbled with my button, but when he finally took hold of me, he groaned.

"Feel how hard you make me?" I asked.

His eyes flashed to mine, so uncertain.

I began to stroke him, long and hard. "You feel amazing," I murmured.

He slid my dick in his fist and he was thrusting into my hand. I kissed him, all lips and tongue, and he made a whining noise that sounded like a plea.

So I pumped him a little harder, kissed him a little deeper, and he began to tremble. His ministrations on my cock became harder; he squeezed and I bucked into his fist. "Fuck yeah," I ground out. "You're gonna make me come."

His cock pulsed in my hand, swelling hot and impossibly hard before he went rigid. He bucked one final time and came, his face a mask of ecstasy as his orgasm took hold of him.

The sight of him and the smell of sex was all it took for me. He still had my cock in his hand but he was too blissed out to finish me off, so I slid my hand over his and we did it together. Just a few pumps was all it took, and when my senses came back to me, Richard was staring at me, looking at my face, my cock in our joined hands, and where my come had shot onto his belly.

He was so fucking hot. I couldn't help it. I rolled us over, me on top of him, and kissed him for all he was worth.

Our cocks were pressed together, spent and sensitive, and he opened his legs and rolled his hips. He gripped my back and angled his head so I could kiss him deeper, and we stayed like that until we needed to breathe. When he pulled his mouth from mine, he rolled us back onto our sides and he snuggled into my neck.

"Thank you," he whispered.

"Thank you, Richard," I replied, kissing the side of his head. "You can recall that anytime you need when you're over there."

"I'll recall every second with you."

We were silent for a while. We knew goodbyes were coming, and I was pretty sure neither one of us wanted to say it.

I'd almost dozed off again when he pulled away and sat up. "I gotta get going," he whispered.

I scrubbed my hands over my face and sat up too. We were a mess. No real shower in three days, covered in dried spunk and ingrained dirt and mud. We redressed the best we could. "My clothes are a mess. They're gonna take one look at me and have me report to the drill sergeant."

I wasn't sure if that was a joke or not. "Can you grab a shower somewhere?"

He shrugged. "I'll figure it out. I might need to find a Laundromat while I'm at it." Then he looked at me and grinned. "I ain't ever been this dirty in my whole life."

I chuckled. "Pretty great, huh?"

"Wouldn't change a thing," he said. Then he frowned. "Except the whole leaving part."

I grabbed my rucksack and rummaged through it for some paper and a pen. I knew I had a notebook in there, and when I found it, I scribbled down my address and our dorm contact phone number, ripped it out, and handed it to him. "Here. Please take this. Write to me, as often as you want. Every day if you can. And be sure to let me know how I can write back, or how I can send it to you. I won't be able to reply if you don't."

He took the piece of paper and stared at the writing before he swallowed hard. "You don't know how much this means to me."

"Promise me you'll write."

He nodded. "I promise."

I smiled. "Good. And I'll keep my promise to you. That when you get back, we'll finish what we started."

He smiled, kinda sadly. Like he didn't want to dare believe me. So I handed him the notebook. "Take this, and the pen," I said, handing that over too. "Now you got no excuses not to write. I'll need you to let me know you're okay, or I'll go crazy with worry."

He smiled a little more genuinely now and shoved the notepad and pen into his bag. He made sure he was somewhat respectable, and we crawled out of the tent.

There were people leaving now, a steady stream of folks walking toward the gates, and cars trying to leave. I guessed they all needed to get back to real life on Monday morning, and I wondered if anyone else was leaving to go fight in a war they didn't believe in. Or if it was just Richard. I wondered who else, how many other young lives might be cut short because of government discourse. But I didn't say that.

I spotted Kathryn, and we made our way over to where she was talking to a group of people. They were laughing, so it looked pleasant enough. "Richard's leaving now," I said.

She turned to him and tried to smile. "Be safe over there."

He swallowed thickly. "I will."

Then she turned to one of the guys she'd been talking to. "Hey, take some photographs of my friends," she said. She stood beside me and we faced the photographer. "Stand in nice and close," she instructed us, so the three of us each had our arms around each other's backs. Then she stepped away and said, "Now just you two." And I knew what she was doing. She'd orchestrated a way for Richard and me to have our photograph taken together.

The photographer snapped away, and Kat gave me a knowing smile. She could be a driven political force when she wanted to be, but there was a reason why she was my friend.

"Okay then," she said. "Richard, you take care."

He gave a nod, and then it was just us two and a goodbye that felt unbearable to say. We walked with the departing crowd for a bit, and I heard someone mention a bus. "Hey, are there buses leaving?" I asked.

"Yeah," she replied. "From Bethel."

"To New York City?" I asked.

She smiled and nodded. "I think so. Pretty sure that's what they said. They brought in special buses."

A car was passing us, not much faster than walking pace, filled on the inside, and there were two guys sitting on the trunk. "Hey, we're going to Bethel if you want to jump on," one said. He was clearly still stoned, talking slow and smiling wide. "We're all beautiful people."

Richard looked at me, unsure. He needed to leave, and a lift was better than walking the whole way. "Go," I said.

He froze for a bit, then hugged me, so hard, for the longest few seconds. "I'm scared," he whispered.

"Don't be. I want your first letter to be a list of all the things we're gonna do when you get back, okay?"

He nodded against me, then without a goodbye, he ran after the car and jumped up on the trunk. He sat facing me, his bag in his lap, and I stood there and watched him until the car was so far away I couldn't see him anymore while Joe Cocker sang about getting by with a little help from his friends.

I raised my hand to wave goodbye, and then, like the universe felt the ache in my heart, it began to rain.

LETTERS

August 20, 1969

DEAR G,

I'm writing to you from the plane, somewhere in the sky between America and Vietnam. I've never flown across the ocean before. I'm trying really hard not to think of how far I am off the water.

After I left you, I made it to Bethel and had a shower there, thankful I didn't have to sit on a bus in the state I was in. I looked a mess, and I was pretty sure no bus driver would've wanted me on their bus looking or smelling the way I did. I got to wash my clothes in New York City. I've never seen a place like it. I thought there were a lot of people at Woodstock but boy, was I wrong. It was an amazing city, and I'd like to get back there one day. I saw LA from the air and the army barracks. I'd like to see more of it one day too.

Which brings me to your request. A list of all the things I'd like to do when I get back. Okay, so here goes:

I'd like to spend more time in big cities. New York would be nice, but I don't think it would matter much where it was. As long as I was with you.

I want to try new things. Food I wouldn't normally eat, restaurants I wouldn't normally go to, movies I wouldn't normally watch, books I wouldn't think to read.

I want to go hiking like you mentioned.

I want to see other things I've never seen before.

I want to put my feet in the Pacific Ocean.

I want a job where I make a difference. Not on my dad's farm. I want more from life than that.

I wanted you to know how much this last weekend meant to me. I'm so used to being miserable on the inside, not being true to myself. But you showed me a whole world I never knew existed. You showed me where I'm supposed to belong. By taking a chance and saying hello to me in that diner, you changed my life, and I'll be forever grateful.

I'd also like to do a whole lot more of what we did in your tent. I want to hear all about what you do at college and your dreams for the future. I want to know everything about you.

Well, this got kind of long, sorry. We're flying into an airbase near Saigon, and from there to some undisclosed location. I'm not sure when I'll be able to write next or how often, but I will try. I made a promise to write and I intend to keep it.

They gave us all a slip with our postal addresses on it. I'll add it to the envelope for you. I don't expect anyone else to write, so you may as well have it. I have no idea what to expect when we land. There's talk that we're heading north, but I can't say for sure. Just so you know, I'm in the C Company, 5th battalion, 3rd platoon.

I can't deny that I'm scared. But I will see this through, and when I get back, we can see about making a start on this list. The funny thing is, I wasn't sure if I ever intended to come back. Not saying I came here to die, but if that did happen, well… it might have been an easier way out instead of living life in hell. But now, I don't have to live a life pretending to be somebody I'm not. Those three short days when I was with you was the freest I have ever been. And it's been a long time since I've looked forward to anything, but I'm excited about what life might be like when I get back.

I haven't even arrived and I'm already thinking about leaving.

I hope you can find time to write back. And I hope you don't mind I signed this letter to G. Just in case the wrong eyes read it. I know you understand.

Yours,

R

September 12, 1969

DEAREST R,

I was so excited to get your letter. It was postmarked Saigon, so I knew you had arrived. I was so relieved that you got there safely, which is silly really, given the dangers you must face now you're there.

Of course, I was going to write back. I told you I would. I promised. And I always keep my promises. Our weekend at Woodstock meant a lot to me, and watching you leave affected me more than I thought it would. I wasn't prepared for how much it would hurt. Kat found me standing in the rain. I hadn't moved from the spot where I stood to wave goodbye. She took me and fed me and we watched more bands right through to the morning. It rained again and a lot of people left, but we watched Jimi Hendrix sing a version of the "Star Spangled Banner," and it blew everyone's mind. I wish you could've seen it.

We made our way back to Connecticut, and Pauly and I slept for two days. I missed some classes, and a few professors weren't happy but I don't regret a thing. Except for you leaving, of course. I regret that the most.

It was hard to read about you thinking about not coming back, but I'm glad you told me. I don't want you to think you can't tell me anything. Any thought, any fear, you can always tell me. You don't have to pretend to be anything you're not for me. And I'm glad now that you're thinking about the future. We have that list of yours to get through! I'm looking forward to all of it.

What I'm doing at college is pretty boring compared to what you're doing. I'm studying business management and economics. Not sure where I'll end up with it, corporate or in the private sector. I realize it would probably bore most people to sleep, but I find it all kinda interesting. The campus itself is really pretty, and everyone is cool. I'd love to know what it looks like where you are. I see pictures on the news but I bet it doesn't do it justice. I never used to be too concerned with the news, but now I find myself watching it, waiting for anything on Vietnam, and when they show helicopters and soldiers and injured people, I wonder if that's where you are.

I sure hope it's not.

So I guess this letter is a bit of a test in seeing how long it takes to find you, or if it finds you at all. You take care of yourself, keep your head down, and please don't go stopping any bullets with your body.

Yours,

G

October 4, 1969

DEAREST G,

I have never been so grateful to get mail in all my life. I can't explain how much your reply means to me. Just to hear of home… We call anything to do with home 'the world' because here feels like we're so far removed from everything. And to hold something in my hands that came from the world was the best feeling, but knowing it came from you? I don't have the words to describe it.

Getting letters from the world is such a boost to all the guys. And I felt very honored that you had written back to me.

The group of guys I'm with is okay, some more than others. I made friends with Karel Rodriguez. He's from Louisiana, and he's a real nice guy. He got a letter from his girl the same day I got your letter, and he is smiling as he is writing back to her, much like I probably am too.

At the time of writing this, we're stationed just outside of Rach Kein. Our division has been designated to help rebuild a road. We have to do sweeps, and we're on a rotating roster. I'm with Karel for most everything we do, and I'm grateful for him. We keep each other sane in a crazy place.

It's hard to describe it here. There is such beauty. The ocean and the beaches as we flew over were a blue I've never seen before. The jungle, the trees, the grass, everything is really green. But there's a lot of devastation here as well. I can't help but think how different it would be if this war was on home soil. We wouldn't be so careless, so unforgiving. We haven't seen any direct combat yet, but our CO said our time would come.

It's hot here, and it's not even summer yet. But it's a tropical heat, and the sweat just runs out of you. Even the nights are warm. And the rain. Holy hell, I ain't seen nothing like it. One good thing about the rain is that it keeps the mosquitoes away. While it's raining, anyway. They're almost as big as the birds. We have to take malaria pills, and we can't drink the water. Some nights we sleep on the ground. Captain Daniels, he was a squad leader with the Delta, has been here for two years, and when he was down south last summer, he said one night they heard a tiger roar from somewhere in the jungle. How crazy is that?

I don't know how long we'll be here. I'm pretty sure we'll be moving all the time, just a few weeks in the one spot at the most. But the address I gave you will find me, no matter where we are.

I think of you a lot.

I wonder what time it is there. If you're awake or asleep. And if you think of me.

I haven't even sent this yet, and I'm already looking forward to your reply. Oh, and I'll do my best not to stop any bullets with my body.

Yours,

R

October 25, 1969

DEAREST R

I hope reading this letter makes you as happy as the first one did. I have to admit I was the same when I saw an envelope from you today. Pauly said my smile was embarrassing. He also said to say hello, and he hopes you're keeping well over there.

Remember how that guy at Woodstock took our photograph with Kat, just before you left. He works for her college newspaper. Anyway, Kat gave me them the other day. I thought you might like to keep one, so I've added it in the envelope. Keep it close to your heart. It's where I keep yours.

I love that photo. It really captured the moment, and you're just as handsome as I remember. I have to admit, seeing you in that picture took my breath away, and my heart aches knowing you're half a world away.

I don't know what else you want to know about me, so I'll start with some random facts. I have an older sister, Marie. She's married now and living in West Hartford. My favorite color is green. I like strawberry shakes over chocolate, and my favorite time of year is spring. When I was growing up, I had a dog named Polly, and my dad always said the dog was mad because we named it after a parrot. My favorite smell is the coming of rain, and I hate green beans. Tell me all the random facts about you.

I hope you're keeping safe. I watch the news every chance I get, sometimes two or three times a night. The newspapers don't cover much more than the politics, but I still scan the grainy photographs for your face. The news replays old footage, but I still watch it. And every time they pause to read the names of the fallen, I don't breathe until the end, and then I feel guilty for being thankful it was someone else instead of you.

Everyone's planning Halloween parties, and I've enrolled in additional classes in the spring quarter. So I'm keeping busy, but I think of you all the time. You wondered if I thought of you… rest assured, I do. When you lie down on the ground tonight, or wherever it is you manage to sleep, know someone on the other side of the planet is sending up prayers for you. I've never been very religious, but I figure it can't hurt.

Kat and Lyman are heading to Washington DC next month to take part in some big anti-war protests. Of course they wanted me to go with them. And maybe before I met you I might have gone, but it's different now, because of you. I'm not for the war, and I wish it was all over, but I couldn't in my right mind protest against something that involves you. Kat said she understood, but Lyman was mad. I'm not bothered though. I'm a live-and-let-live kind of person, and I'd rather him be mad at me than feel like I'm doing you a disservice.

Am I allowed to send packages to you? Or just letters? I was thinking you might like some candy or something that tastes like home. Is there anything you miss the most? Let me know and I'll get it to you somehow.

I hope you like the photo, and I hope you're allowed to keep it.

Please keep your head down, and remember, no stopping bullets with your body. Say hello to your buddy Karel for me. And for what it's worth, I'm glad you have a friend over there.

I eagerly await your reply,

Yours,

G

November 16, 1969

DEAREST G,

Your letter today couldn't have come at a better time. We headed north after my last letter, and it hasn't been easy. We've reached Binh Phuoc and will be here a while. We came under enemy fire, and suddenly being here got very real. Since I arrived, I felt kind of removed from the war. I mean, there are always helicopters and gunfire in the distance, and minesweeping, but nothing like this.

It was the second platoon, another US unit, that saved our asses, and we've joined forces to hold this location. They're okay. They've been here longer, some of them on their second or third tour. I can't even imagine that. The stories they tell. G, it's… it's the stuff of nightmares. You can see it in their eyes. They get a blank, faraway look, and it scares me.

Anyway, sorry for being such a downer. It's just hard here. Like I said, your letter arriving was a much-needed lift to my spirits.

And the photograph…

The photograph brought tears to my eyes. I had to step

away so the guys wouldn't see, but Karel kept watch of me. He asked if I'd received bad news, but I told him it was the opposite. I showed him the photo, telling him you were a dear childhood friend. It felt wrong to lie, but I can't tell the truth. They can't know. If anyone found out…

Karel said he understood. He misses home too, and his mom sent a photo of her and his brother, and it upset him.

I sent my parents a letter to let them know I'd arrived, and they replied once. Just a few lines. I don't know what I expected or why I keep expecting more when I know I'll never get it. Not from them. I haven't written back to them. If and when I get news about leaving, maybe I'll let them know.

It still rains a lot. It comes down like buckets, and sometimes we have to walk through fields with water up to our waists. If it's not water, it's mud, and my feet hurt. I don't think they've been dry for weeks. They keep warning us not to get foot rot, but there's not much else we can do.

Of course you can send care packages. Guys get them every so often. It makes everyone happy just to see the smiles when they get something from home. I don't know what I miss the most. I'm craving a burger and fries, but I don't think that would mail too well sitting in a box for a few weeks. Ha!

Most of the guys here get sent gum or taffy. I guess it ships well. Or maybe you've got some leftover Halloween candy. I don't really mind. It's your letters I like the most.

Our CO said he might try to get us a special dinner for Thanksgiving, but I'll believe it when I see it. Are you going back home for Thanksgiving? I hope you have a real nice time. Have a double serving of turkey for me. Extra cranberry sauce, please!

I guess it will be getting cold there now. It's hotter than hell here. When it's not raining, the air is so thick it's hard to breathe. I'd much rather be shoveling snow in driveways.

I've been here for almost three months. It feels like a lifetime.

I think about you every day. Especially at nighttime. I don't sleep much, so thinking about you, what you might be up to, helps pass the time.

Oh, some random facts about to me. I like chocolate milkshakes over strawberry, my favorite time of year is fall. I grew up on a farm, so I had a bunch of animals as pets. Dogs, cats, birds, rabbits. Dogs are my favorite though. Don't know if I have a favorite smell, but when the crabapple trees are in blossom, it makes me think of my grandma. Her garden in spring was always beautiful. My favorite food of all time is a homemade apple pie, and my least favorite thing is Jell-O. No food should wobble. It's not right.

I look forward to your next letter. More than I can say.

Yours,

R

December 25, 1969

MY DEAREST R,

Today is Christmas Day, and while I spent it with my family, my heart is a few thousand miles away on the other side of the world.

I keep thinking about what you're doing, or where you are, or if you're safe. I wish you were here. I kept being distracted by the news until my mom asked me why. So I told her. I told her about you and about how I worry and how I wish it would all end so you could come home.

She took the news well and was even a little bit excited for me, that I found someone I care about. I told her how we met, minus some details, of course, and how we've been writing for months. I told her you were someone special and that one day when you get back, I'd like her to meet you. I hope that doesn't scare you. Don't be too afraid about it. She just wants me to be happy, and if that includes you, then that's fine with her.

She's not a fan of the war. Not for any political reason. She just hates knowing that there's a whole lotta moms out there without their sons. She cries when they read the names of the fallen. She weeps for the parents who lose their children.

I know this is your first Christmas away from home, and I can only imagine how hard it is for you. Hope your CO managed to get your Thanksgiving dinner, and I hope you arrange something for Christmas as well.

Next year, I'm gonna make your Christmas the best one ever. Just you wait and see. We'll have turkey and all the trimmings and gifts and wood fires. I'll make it one you will never forget. That's another promise.

And I keep my promises.

So I put together a little care package. It's just mostly things I thought you might like. It's a shame you won't get it in time for your Christmas. I hope it all arrives in one piece, and I hope it lifts your spirits. My mom made tiny individual Christmas fruitcakes, and she insisted that I send one. I won't be offended if you don't eat it. I don't like fruitcake much. But she insisted, so I added it to the box.

Another random fact about me. My birthday is July twenty-fourth and next year I'll be twenty-two. The only gift I want this year is for you to come home. I want to see your smile and hear you laugh. Nothing else will do.

I still watch the news, hoping to see a glimpse of your face. I read the newspapers too, looking for places you've mentioned. I don't know where you are now or what places you've seen. I pray you've seen no more enemy fire, and I pray you come home safe. You have to now, because my mom wants to meet you, and she said you have to come home safe and sound, and what she says, goes. That's just how it is.

I'm just joking around. But she really does want you to be safe.

And so do I.

I look at your photo every day.

Merry Christmas, Richard. And happy New Year. Let's hope the new decade will bring a change of peace. And the very best part about this coming new year is that this is the year you come home. I'm counting down the days.

All my love,

G

January 21, 1970

DEAREST G,

I got my package today! Thank you so much! It was like all my Christmases came at once. The taffy and gum are a real treat, thank you. I almost had to fight some of the guys for the socks. I can't believe you thought to send some. Our army-issued socks are more holes than sock, and these were truly appreciated. Thank you. The cookies too! Sure beats the C rations we get here.

Please tell your mom the Christmas cake was the best I ever ate. I shared it with Karel. It only seemed right to do so, and he said it tasted like home. Please tell her I said thank you from the bottom of my heart.

I can't believe you told her about me! I'm stunned, but also incredibly happy. I know it seems crazy, but it's like a confirmation that what I feel is real. And that you feel it too. I can't imagine telling my parents, which I realize is incredibly unfair to you. But I hope you can see that's a reflection on them and not on my feelings for you. I haven't heard any more from my folks. Can't say I'm surprised.

Again, tell your mom I said thanks. She sounds like an incredible person. Like you.

You have kept me sane here, whether you realize it or not. Some days when things are bad, it's thinking about you and rereading your letters and looking at your photograph that gets me through.

You're like my lifeline.

We're stationed west of Binh Phuoc. We still sweep the roads, and we've helped rebuild some houses and a hospital. But we're pushing the VC back. We've come under enemy fire now more times than I can count. The jungle is thick here and kind of swampy. It makes for real hard going. We've lost two men in our unit, both shot near me. I can still hear the screaming, G. I don't think I'll ever forget it. Karel said he had a bullet go past his ear, so close it grazed him. Scared me to death.

I don't mean to cause you to worry. And I'm working on not stopping any bullets with my body every day. So far, so good.

It's starting to cool off now, and it doesn't rain every day like it did. But the nights are colder, and sleeping on the ground really is the pits. Not that we sleep much. We have to sleep half-awake because the VC own the night. I'm starting to wonder if I'll ever sleep more than an hour at a time ever again.

Thanks again for the package. Words cannot describe how much it means. I'm sad I won't be there for your birthday. I know next year feels like a lifetime away, but maybe next year I can make it up to you.

All my love as well,

R

February 14, 1970

DEAREST R,

Would you believe I got your letter on Valentine's Day? It's the best Valentine's Day present I could have asked for. I'm sorry you're having such a terrible time, and I wish the war would end and you could come home early. I wish for it every day.

But you should be home just in time for your birthday. I promise I'll make that special for you. Anything you want, just name it, and if it's within my power to see it done, then I will.

Of course I told my mom about you! You're constantly in my thoughts, every day and every night. Especially at night, if you know what I mean. I told my mom that yes, it's crazy because we just met. We only had one weekend together, but through our letters, I feel you know me better than anyone else. I told her I've fallen in love with you. And when you wrote about how you feel about me, I hope it's love you feel for me too.

I want you to know I'm not seeing anyone else. There

hasn't been anyone else. You captured my heart that day back in August, and I don't want anyone else but you.

And I'm honored that you think about me, to help you get through tough times over there. I can't imagine what you're going through. I still watch the news, and I see the guns and the helicopters and the injuries, and I still can't imagine it.

I can't imagine the fear you feel.

College is taking up the majority of my time now. It's only three months until I graduate! That's exciting and scary at the same time. So all of my time is taken up with research and study, and when I'm not at the library being a total book buster, I'm thinking about you.

I looked up where Binh Phuoc was on a map. Wow. Kinda doesn't seem real that you're so far away, but when I see it on a map, it brings it home. You really are on the other side of the world. I'm grateful for our letters; they keep me sane as well. I watch the calendar waiting for each reply. Around the three-week mark and every day over that, I have a lump of dread in my belly.

If your letter is just a day or two late, I become sick with worry.

In light of Valentine's Day, I'm putting together another small package. Even though it's nothing too exciting, I hope it brings you some comfort. I like the idea of you getting small gifts. It doesn't have to be a birthday or Christmas. I would do it for no other reason than to perhaps put a smile on your face.

I'm sorry your parents haven't replied. I wish they could see what a remarkable man you are. I wish they knew you didn't have to go to war to prove that you're brave. The man who took a chance at Woodstock, who made a list of all the things he'd never done and checked each one off, the man who finally saw that he deserved to be happy. That takes more courage than most men are capable of. Don't ever forget that.

We had a big snowstorm, which must seem a world away from you right now. Maybe when you get back in time for winter we can make some snow angels and a snowman. Then maybe thaw out together in front of the fire...

Well, I hope you enjoy the care package I put together for you. Please take care, and make sure you come home to me.

All my love,

G

March 8, 1970

DEAREST G,

Your care package was amazing, and very much appreciated. You said that it was nothing too exciting, but I'm telling you, it's better than birthdays and Christmases combined. And knowing you do it for no other reason than to make me happy, to bring me comfort, well that makes it even better.

But your letter made me the happiest guy in the world. Seeing your words, written by your own hand, telling me that you have fallen in love with me makes me so happy I could burst.

At Woodstock, you showed me that it was possible. That I could be happy, that I could find someone who would understand and would want to be with me. I never even thought that was possible. I thought it was something I didn't deserve. But to love someone and have them love you in return, it's not something I thought I would ever have.

I fell in love with you when you sat down across from me in that diner. When you asked me to come with you and your group of friends. When you changed my life. Right then. Maybe I didn't know at the time, but I can see in hindsight when you said hello to me that very first time, my heart was yours. You made me feel like I could do anything, and you looked at me like no one ever had.

You saw the real me.

We're still at Binh Phuoc. We had to rebuild the bridge, and it's almost done. We have constant attacks from the VC, usually at nighttime but not always. There's a constant noise of helicopters and M16's, and we're so used to it now that if there's just a moment of silence, we'll stop and stare at each other like something is really wrong. It's eerie as hell. When bombs go off in the distance and the gunfire starts again, it's almost a relief.

Crazy, huh?

Before I got here, I'd never even been in a helicopter, now we go all the time. We run patrols looking for camps. The crazy thing about the NVA is that we can hear their guns, and sometimes an order shouted through the jungle, but you can't see them. Sometimes at night if the wind is right, we can smell their campfires. It plays with your head.

We got reports of another company that had it really bad. They got pinned down the other day and nine more killed and thirty wounded. Our unit has five injured and four dead, and we're counted as the lucky ones.

I've enclosed a photo. Mike has a camera and he has to send it home to get the photos developed. This photo is of a few of the guys from my squad. I'm on the far left, and that's Karel next to me. I thought you might like it. I know I look skinny; my belt's on the smallest hole now. We don't get real food very often. Everything is either canned or freeze-dried. Maybe that's why the cookies you send taste like they're from heaven.

I wish I could be there to see you graduate. And I wish more than anything I could be there for your birthday.

Please know you're in my heart and in every waking thought.

All my love,

R

April 2, 1970

DEAREST R,

My days are filled with exams, and I spend my night times studying. It helps pass the time. Everyone's excited about graduation, my mom and dad especially. And my sister and her husband are expecting their first baby, which is some much-needed good news.

I loved the photo you sent. And yes, you look skinny as hell. Just means we'll have to spend a good time feeding you when you get home.

You'll be pleased to know Pauly transferred to MIT. I was sad to see him go, but he needed to. He assured me he already sourced the best weed in Boston and made friends with a few of the math geeks in a matter of days.

Lyman's headed for Washington like we all knew he would. His passion for politics might have driven us all crazy at times but he's the kind of guy who will make changes.

The big surprise is that Kathryn isn't going with him. She said it's been coming for a while, and it's amicable for the most part, but since they split, she and I have become close. She has some affiliate course link to Stanford in California. There's some big technology movement going to boom soon, and she's heading there in June.

She's asked me to go with her, and Richard, I'm considering it. It's a great opportunity and they want a young start-up group, and with my business management degree, it's kinda perfect.

San Francisco is where it's all happening. And don't for one minute think this plan doesn't include you. It's up to you, of course, and depends on where you see yourself returning to, but this is your official invitation to join us.

I know it's crazy to think about, and you have your parents' farm in New York, but if you want, you can come stay with me. I don't even know where I'll be living yet or if Kat and I will be roommates, but the offer for you is there.

I would love nothing more.

Anyway, we can talk about that later. And maybe you might want to go straight to see your parents first. And maybe you don't want to ever live in California, but please, can we talk about it before you say no? I wouldn't be leaving for about two months yet, so we have plenty of time.

We just have to get you home first. I can't help but picture sunny weekends together. You and me.

Please just say you'll think about it.

I'm sending another care package. I didn't realize just how much they meant to you. They don't cost much to put together, and if it makes you happy, then it's worth every penny.

All my love,

G

May 5, 1970

DEAREST G,

Sorry it's taken me so long to reply. Things have been bad here. The war's been hell. I can't describe it any other way. We've moved farther northwest and have taken position on higher ground. All the allied bases have been hit pretty bad and this keeps the choppers out of the sky. We've got no mail, no food, no water, no supplies at all, because every time a chopper tries to get into us, they become targets. The VC have hit every unit around us, and there are air strikes in the valleys below us all the time. Some bombs are just background noise, and some sound like freight trains.

It doesn't seem to matter how many times we bomb them, they never seem to stop. Makes me wonder if they'll ever stop. Or how many men have to die before this is all over.

We have new guys shipped in every couple of weeks. They're so woefully unprepared, and the fresh horror on their faces when they see so much death just kills me. I know I must've been the same when I first got here. That feels like a lifetime ago.

I've been promoted to squad leader, which should be something worth celebrating if it didn't scare me so much. Seems the only thing you have to do to get promoted in the army is not die. There's only a handful of our original squad left. Karel is still with me, and that's a blessing. When we get notified of which units have been hit, with the names of those guys who didn't make it, I don't even cry anymore.

When they clear the north side of the mountain, down into the valley, we'll be on the move again. The jungle is so thick through there you can't see the sun, and at the bottom is a river we'll need to cross by rope. Then there will be another stroll through miles of jungle on the other side. It's not just the VC we need to look out for, but mosquitoes and leeches as well. I also now have to worry about the men I'm responsible for. Not only does their inexperience make a liability of my life, but my lack of experience could cost them theirs.

I don't know which is worse.

So, San Francisco, huh?

I've never been, but I've heard it's pretty cool. I'm not sure what to say about your invitation. I just want to see you, and I guess that it doesn't matter whether it's in Connecticut or in California. I don't know how things will be with my parents. Have written to them twice, and they've replied but only a few lines each time, and each reply is the same as any conversation I've ever had with them. Only ever about the farm, the weather, and the folks at church. They don't ask how I am and don't tell me to be safe, and they don't say they wish I'll come home. They don't say they miss me because the truth is, I'm guessing they don't.

So perhaps I can come to San Francisco and stay a while, and we can take it from there. If I leave my ticket open-ended, I could stay for a week, or a month, or forever. You might decide I'm not the man you remembered. This place has changed me. I know it has. But it has also solidified something for me. That life is too short to be unhappy.

I want to see you so bad. I want to feel your arms around me, and I want to hear the beat of your heart when you hold me against you. But mostly I want to feel safe, and the safest place I've ever been is when I'm with you.

Sorry this letter's a bit of a downer. And sorry for the state of the paper. My hand keeps smearing dirt as I write. We haven't been able to shower for a while.

I miss you like I didn't think was possible. And it scares me that I'm not the man you met all those months ago anymore, and that maybe this war has messed me up so much I don't recognize myself.

Wish I were coming home today.

All my love,

R

May 28, 1970

DEAREST R,

It was such a nice surprise to get your letter a few days early. I'm sending you another care package. It's just some treats and some coffee, and Harvey Corbett from a room down the hall in my dorm was packing up and he had a bunch of comics. He was just gonna toss them out, so I grabbed them for you. I hope that takes your mind off the terrible things that are happening over there.

I still watch the news, keeping an ear out for any of the locations that you mention. I saw there was a lot of fighting near where you were the other month, and I hope to God you didn't go back there. They said that fifteen were dead and forty injured, and I listened for your name. It makes me feel so sick to my stomach that I almost want to puke.

I wish you were coming home today too.

Graduation is next week. I can't believe college is over. It's been an awesome experience but I'm looking forward to what comes next. I'm still hoping that my future includes you. We'll have so much to talk about when you get home, but there's no rush. I meant it when I said I love you, and I know commitment can be a scary thing but we can take it one day at a time.

I don't know if you get much news over there, but there's been more protests about the war. I can't make myself go. It feels wrong, as though I'm betraying you somehow. If I thought standing out there with a picket sign would bring you home any sooner, I would do it every day. But the government doesn't care. I wish people could understand it wasn't the soldiers who started the war. So don't listen to the naysayers. I want you to know that I'm proud of you for serving our country so that we can be free. And congratulations on the promotion!

You have sacrificed so much, and I am incredibly proud of you.

It looks like the move to San Francisco is happening. It's kind of exciting even though it's scary at the same time. I should have everything in the apartment set up by the time you get home, so all you will need to bring is yourself and a change of clothes. We can take day trips up and down the coast, stopping wherever you want. We can spend some days at the beach, and in winter, nights in front of the fire. You can probably tell I've been daydreaming.

We have the rest of our lives to be together, and I cannot wait to start.

Miss you more each day. All my love,

G

June 28, 1970

DEAREST R,

It's been four weeks and I still have had no reply. I hope to God you're okay. I've watched the news from all over the country, read any newspaper I could find looking for any detail on a familiar location or a name. But there's been nothing. Maybe the choppers were delayed again and they can't get the mail out. That's what I'm telling myself. Anything else is just too hard to imagine.

I'm staying with my parents for a few days before the big move west. Don't worry about the change of address because all my mail from college is still being forwarded to my folks, and my mom's going to send it on once we get settled. She promised me she will call me if I get any mail from you. She knows how worried I am. She worries for you too.

Kat and I are leaving in three days. We're gonna drive across country in her trusty blue van from Woodstock. Keeping my fingers crossed to hear from you before I leave.

I'm praying for you every night, and I think about you every minute of every day.

Please write when you can.

All my love,

G

July 10, 1970

DEAREST R,

Still no word from you, and I'm terribly worried. I've tried everything I can think of to find out any information, but I meet one dead end after another.

I'm adding my new phone number and address, but my mom assures me there's been no mail. My heart is breaking with worry.

San Francisco is fine. Summer is warm, but there's a breeze off the ocean. Though I can't enjoy it because my mind keeps wandering back to you. This was going to be our new life together, and the idea of being here without you doesn't feel right.

I feel like everything is out of step. And not knowing is the worst! I just wish I knew what was going on or what happened, but then I realize maybe I don't want to know. Because knowing, hearing someone say out loud that you're not coming home would make it real.

It would make it unbearable.

I don't know what else to do.

Please God, let you be all right.
I'll never give up on you.
All my love,
G

Three days later...

GARY

"STILL NOTHING?" Kat asked.

I closed the newspaper, blinking back tears. "There's no mention of his division, his platoon, his location. Nothing. Mom's read all the papers from back home and there's nothing."

"And you've called the army number?" she asked.

"I could call them a dozen times and it won't change the fact I'm not family. They won't tell me anything."

Kat sat down at the table with me, frowning. She squeezed my hand. "What about his actual family? His parents?"

"And tell them what? That I'm his boyfriend and I'm worried sick?"

"No. Tell them you're a classmate or a friend from training who came home already."

"I can't lie to his parents. They don't even seem to like him too much, let alone some strange man who calls looking for him. His dad already suspects that Richard's gay, and that's why he went to Vietnam in the first place."

"Then I'll call them."

I stared at her. "You would?"

"And if they won't tell me, then I'll call the local store or the diner you found him in. Maybe someone there knows something. You know how small towns like to talk."

Twenty minutes and two different switchboard directories later, Kat had a number. She was put through. She covered the mouthpiece with her hand. "It's ringing."

My nerves were about to give out, and my stomach was in knots. I held my breath.

"Yes, hello," Kat said. "Is this Mrs. Ronsman? … My name is Linda and I went to school with Richard. We exchanged some letters while he's been away in Vietnam, but I haven't had a reply for a while now and I'm sick with worry. … Yes, that's right. Linda Bentford. … No, he was in the year above me…"

Kat frowned and I thought for one dreadful moment that our ruse had been found out, and we were going to meet another dead end. But then Kat snatched up my pen and scribbled across the newspaper.

Telegram. Injured.

Then she started to write something but scribbled it out. Then she wrote *Balboa Hospital, San Diego.*

"Oh my," Kat said, more politely than I'd ever heard her speak. "Is it serious? Will he be okay?"

But I didn't hear anything else. My head was swimming and the room tilted and the world started to turn again.

He was alive.

He was in the US.

HE WAS ALIVE.

AND THEN THE TEARS STARTED.

"He's alive?" I croaked out.

She nodded, teary-eyed too. I hadn't realized she'd hung the phone up. "His leg is shattered pretty bad. His mom didn't know when he'd be out. They haven't been to see him; can't leave the farm apparently."

"I'm going," I said, standing up.

Kat blinked and looked up at me. "What? Now?"

"Right now. I can take the next flight and be there before dinner."

"Do you think you should call first?"

I probably should, but I was already packing.

I heard Kat sigh from the living room and mumble about taking time off work. I stuck my head around the door. "What are you talking about?"

She raised an eyebrow at me. "You don't think I'm letting you go alone?"

I gave her a grateful smile. "Thank you."

She waved me off and was already on the phone again, asking directory assistance for the phone number of the airport.

WE WERE on the next flight to San Diego. I was grateful Kat was coming with me. She didn't want me to go alone, but she also thought we might need a fake girlfriend in the mix to seem less suspicious.

I hated that she was right.

Kat put her hand on my arm as we arrived at the hospital. "Gary, just wait. Take a breath. I know you're excited to see him, but did you stop to wonder why he didn't call you?"

"He didn't have my new number in San Francisco. He didn't have my parents' number back home. He would have been back here after we left college, and who knows, maybe he left Vietnam without any of his things. If he was injured so bad and they choppered him out right then and there—"

"Okay," she conceded. "I just don't want you to be hurt."

"I need to see him regardless. If he doesn't want to see me, then at least I'll know."

She squeezed my arm and we got out of the taxi and made our way to the main doors. The reception area was like most hospitals, but the doors beyond had an army officer with MP on his arm at the entrance. The lady behind the glass window glanced up at us and smiled. "Can I help you?"

I froze. If I couldn't see him… If I'd come all this way…

"Yes, hello," Kat said. "We're here to see Richard Ronsman."

The woman didn't even blink. "Your relation to the patient?"

"He's my brother," Kat answered like it was the God-given truth. She put her hand on my arm. "This is my husband, Gary. We've come from San Francisco."

"One moment, please." The lady took a file and disappeared through another door. The guard at the door eyed us, and Kat gave him a natural smile whereas I was close to going ape.

"Thank God you're here," I whispered to her.

She smiled and gave me a side-on cuddle. "We're close."

"So close I can't stand it."

The reception lady reappeared, her white uniform and

white shoes in pristine order. She smiled. "This way, please."

Oh God, it was really happening.

We were ushered down a corridor, then another, to a set of double doors where another nurse took us into the room. It was a huge open-ward room and it was lined with beds down both sides and an aisle; some beds were partitioned off, some weren't. There must have been forty beds in the room. Each bed had a man in it, with all different kinds of injuries. Some had their heads bandaged, some were torsos of bandages, some had only one arm or one leg. There were televisions on but it was otherwise kind of quiet. Three other men had visitors, and I was trying to scan faces of the men, looking for him.

The nurse stopped walking, nodded toward the last bed, and gave us a curt smile. "Visiting time ends in one hour," she said.

And there he was.

He was lying down, covered with a sheet and one of those blanket support things over his left leg to keep the sheet and blanket off him. He looked at us, then looked again, his eyes falling on me like he couldn't believe it. And his smile…

His whole face lit up, and I knew then, no matter what we had to overcome, that we'd get through it. He started to cry and scrubbed at his face, then tried to sit up and winced at his leg.

"Hey, stay there," I said, going straight to him. I put my hands on his shoulders to keep him still, but then it became a hug and he clung to me. Fisting my shirt, he sobbed into my neck, and I sat on his bed and held him as he cried. Kat stood at the end of the bed and cried too, and I just held him until his tears dried up. "I'm here. I'm here."

He scrubbed at his face and laughed. "I can't believe it's you," he croaked.

The truth was he looked terrible. He's lost so much weight, his face was gaunt, like his eyes and teeth were too big for his head. His hair was longer, shaggy and down over his ears, and there was a haunted look in his eyes. "You can believe it," I said gently. "After all this time, I finally found you."

I stayed seated on his bed and took his hand. Kat walked to the other side, pulled over a chair, and sat beside him, taking his other hand. "Told them I was your sister," she whispered. "And that Gary's my husband."

I squeezed his hand and rubbed his arm. "I only found out where you were this morning. I've been out of my mind with worry," I said. "I called the army a hundred times, but no one would tell me anything. Then Kat had the idea to call your mother."

Richard looked up at me, then to Kat. "You did?"

Kat nodded. "I told her I was a girlfriend from school, and that we'd been writing letters while you were away. I'm sorry I had to lie to her."

He squeezed my hand. "I'm glad you did. I didn't know how to call you, and I wasn't even sure where you were. They shipped me straight home. There was no time to get my gear. I didn't have your address."

"I wrote a few times and never got a reply, and I thought the worst, for sure. I was going out of my mind, and then we found out this morning you were in San Diego, so we boarded the first plane."

Richard looked up at me and smiled, taking in my face like he couldn't believe he was seeing me. "I'm so glad you are here. You have no idea." He swallowed hard. "I haven't had any visitors, and I almost didn't believe it was you."

"Your mom said they hadn't visited because they couldn't leave the farm," Kat said gently.

Richard scoffed. "I'm sure that's what she told you."

"It's okay," I replied. "You've got us."

"I'm sorry for crying all over you," he said, letting go of Kat's hand so he could put his hand to his forehead. "Guess my emotions got the better of me."

"Don't apologize," I said. "You don't ever have to apologize."

"I'm sorry I made you worry. I thought I'd never see you again." He was holding my hand so tight, it almost hurt. "Did you get all moved to San Francisco?"

The guy in the next bed was asleep, so I stole his chair and pulled it up next to Richard's bed. I quickly took his hand again. "It's beautiful. I can't wait for you to see it. You'll love it. We can walk down to the piers, and there are mountains just an hour away where we can go hiking, and we can start crossing off the things on your list."

His guys flashed to mine, then he looked away. "I'm um… I'm a bit of a mess. My leg isn't good, and I don't sleep too well."

"Hey," I said. I threaded our fingers and waited for him to look at me. "I'm pretty sure when I made you that promise, there was no fine print about having two good legs." I smiled at him. "And I didn't make that promise to your leg. I made it to you."

He smiled, all shy like, just the way he did on the day we met. I leaned in real close, making sure no one else could hear. "You're still as cute as the first day we met."

Richard laughed and his cheeks filled with color, then he looked at us both, then looked at me little longer. "I am so glad you're here."

"Me too."

"And you too, Kat. Thank you," he said. "For everything."

"That's fine," she replied. "Someone had to keep Gary from flying to Vietnam to find you."

Richard smiled at that. "Really?"

"Well," I amended. "I was running out of options. I had to find you somehow."

Richard sighed happily, but he was also tired. That much was clear. "My leg is pretty bad. The doctors told me they were going to amputate, but some quick-thinking field medic did such a good job, they thought they'd try and save his handiwork."

"What happened?" I asked quietly.

He licked his lips, and his grip tightened a little, and he did that quick-blinking thing like his mind was taking photographs, seeing horrors I couldn't even imagine.

"We left Binh Phuoc, which was bad enough, but we went to do border patrols of Cambodia. We teamed up with half the Delta boys and our new squad went north to the border. It was some fill-in mission that our CO thought was a good idea. We weren't even supposed to be there." He swallowed hard. "We were doing sweeps and patrols and working shifts, sleeping in holes in the ground, using our gas mask pouches for a pillow. And it rained for a week straight. Rain like you've never seen. Then one morning, just before sunrise, Karel and I went out to do a perimeter check. And it's funny, because I remember thinking the mountains were beautiful that day, then we heard AK fire back at the camp. So we ran back, and the enemy troops were coming out of the jungle. Our radioman got a call out before they shot him, but the chopper took ages. It felt like hours, but I'd lost all sense of time. Anyway, we held them off and pushed them back, but not before they killed half of us. Then we heard the choppers coming in, and I remember thinking it was over, but one of the VC came running in, screaming, then he launched grenades. I broke cover to take him out, but it was too late. Karel tackled me, and he took the brunt of it." He did that quick-blinking thing again. His voice was barely a whisper, his eyes full of tears. His voice was just a whisper. "It caught me in the leg and shattered my thigh, but it got him in the back and the neck. I tried to hold the wound, but there was too much blood. I don't remember the medics screaming at me or the sound of the chopper. I only felt the pain when the doc said the morphine would help."

Jesus Christ.

"Oh, Richard, I'm sorry," I said, crying with him. It was all I could say. I wanted to pull him into my arms and hold him forever. "I'm sorry about Karel. I know how much he meant to you."

"I'm sorry too. He saved my life, but I couldn't save his." He shook his head and tears streamed down his cheeks, and his bottom lip trembled. "I'm not the same man you met at Woodstock. I don't know if I'll ever be the same again."

"Then I'll just have to get to know the new you," I answered. He looked at me like I'd told him the sky wasn't blue. I smiled through my tears. "You can't get rid of me that easy. I'm not going anywhere, okay?"

He began to cry again, like he couldn't let himself believe it.

I leaned in. "Richard, I love you. I'm not going anywhere. I know you've been through hell. You don't need to hide anything from me."

Then he cried again but laughed this time, and he let go of Kat's hand so he could wipe his eyes. He never let go of my hand.

Some dinner ladies wheeled in a cart and a nurse

followed them and came directly to us. I hadn't realized the other visitors had gone. "I'm sorry," she said. "Visiting hours are over."

Richard's hold on my hand tightened. Kat was quick to take his other hand in case she thought anything weird about him holding mine. There was a hint of panic in his eyes, so I was quick to reassure him. "We'll be back tomorrow. I promise. First thing."

"Visiting hours are from nine to eleven," the nurse said. "Then again from three to five."

The dinner lady slid a tray of food onto his bed table, and Richard made a face. The food didn't look that great, and then I noticed what was on it. "He doesn't like Jell-O," I said. "It wobbles."

Richard laughed with fresh tears, his grin wide, and even the nurse smiled. "Well, considering this is the first time I've ever seen Mr. Ronsman smile, you've got five more minutes. Maybe you can convince him to eat something." She gave a wink and turned on her heel and walked out.

I wheeled his table so it bypassed his covered leg and was over his waist. He looked at the food and frowned. "The food here isn't great, but at least it's not C rations," he said.

"I'll be back in the morning. I'll bring you anything you want, just name it. Did you ever get that burger and fries?"

He half smiled and shook his head. "Nah. But I don't reckon bringing that back here would make me too popular with the guys."

"Fair enough," I said. I looked around the room at all the men eating, gave Richard's hand one last squeeze, and held onto it. "We'll leave you to eat in peace, but we'll be back tomorrow."

"Promise?" he asked quickly, like he hadn't meant to say it out loud.

Kat answered first. "Of course we'll be back. Now eat your dinner, we need you strong and healthy."

Then I leaned in and pressed my lips to his temple and whispered to him, "I keep my promises. I'll be here as soon as they open the doors. I love you."

As Kat and I walked out, I looked back at him one more time. He was wiping a tear from his face, but he was still smiling. I waited until we were out the front doors before I let my emotions get the best of me. It was a mix of relief, happiness, love, and a little bit of fear that bottled up inside me and brought tears to my eyes. "Oh my God, he was so happy to see us. I wasn't sure what to expect, but he was happy to see me, right?"

Kat put her hand on my arm. "He was overwhelmed, and it's clear that he is still in love with you."

I knew there was something else she wasn't saying. "But?"

"But he's been through a lot. And when he said he's a mess and that he's not the same man you met all those months ago, I think you should believe him. War does horrible things to people, Gary."

"I know. But I also meant it when I said that I would just get to know the new him. I love him, Kat. I'll help him, and I know it won't be easy."

She gave me a half smile. "I just don't want to see you hurt."

"I know, and thank you. But this feels right." I put my hands to my chest. "In here. I know we're meant to be together."

She smiled more genuinely now. "The nurse said she hadn't seen him smile before. And the way he was looking at you…"

"Like he couldn't believe what he was seeing," I said.

"Like he was scared you were going to disappear or that he was dreaming."

I nodded and it solidified something inside me, and I promised to myself right then that I would never let him down. "Come on, we have a lot to do. I want to buy him some things, and—"

"And how about we find a motel first," Kat said.

Oh. "Right, yes. Good idea. Let's find a room, then we can go shopping."

WE WALKED through the hospital doors at exactly nine o'clock the next morning. I was somehow more excited this time. There was no dread or wondering if he would want to see me. There was no fear of the unknown this time, and I was practically buzzing with anticipation to see him.

And when we walked through the doors to his dorm room, my eyes went straight to the back corner where his bed was. He was sitting up in bed, and his whole face lit up when he saw us. He looked freshly bathed, his hair brushed, clean-shaven, and bright-eyed.

"Someone's happy to see you," the nurse said to Kat. We were still going along with the ruse that Kat was Richard's sister.

Kat smiled at her. "He sure is."

"You look great today," I said, putting the bag of goods on his tray table.

Kat held up the flowers she was holding. "For you," she said, then kissed his cheek first, as a sister should, then I leaned in and gently pressed my lips to his cheek as well.

He seemed a little flushed and nervous. "I wasn't sure if you guys would come today. I know you said you would, but then after you left yesterday, I started to think maybe I dreamed the whole thing."

"No dream," Kat said. "Though going through every aisle in the store three times over could be considered a nightmare."

I sorted out a laugh. "Don't believe her. She loved every minute." I wheeled the tray table toward him, careful of his leg, of course, so he could reach the bag I brought with me. "This is for you."

"All of it?"

"All of it."

"I'm going to see if I can find a vase for the flowers," Kat said, giving us a wink. "Won't be long."

I sat in the chair beside his bed and watched him pull out each item one by one. The first was a writing set, an additional notepad, and a few pens. "So you can write every day," I explained. Then there was a puzzle book, a magazine, and the photo frame with a picture of Kat and me in it. "We found one of those picture booths at the mall. Four for a quarter." I explained. Then I said much quieter, "We thought it would be less conspicuous if it had your sister in it as well, and not just your brother-in-law." I winked.

Richard laughed at that. "I love it, thank you."

"You can keep it on your bedside table," I suggested.

"I will," he said, like he was about to burst.

Next was a tin of cookies and some candy, but also some fresh fruit as well. A pack of cards, two cans of soda, and two dime novels. "I can't believe you bought all of this for me," he said. "I never got this much stuff for all my Christmases combined."

"You deserve more," I answered gently. "I'm sorry your folks haven't been to see you."

Richard shrugged. "I'm not surprised."

I looked around at the closest beds to see if any of the other guys were paying us any attention, but none of them were. "My mom said to say hello," I said, quiet enough. "I called her last night to let her know where I was. And so she would stop worrying. I had her watching the news and reading the papers, trying to help me find my missing soldier."

Richard blushed, and he whispered, "I can't believe you told her about me."

"She wants to meet you."

His eyes went a little wide. "Oh. Yeah, wow."

I laughed and patted his hand. "No pressure."

Kat came back then with a vase with the flowers in it. She put them on his bedside table, then helped him organize his gifts where he could reach them. We talked for a while then about our place in San Francisco, how our new jobs were going, and how we were finding the change of pace. Richard listened intently, smiling and laughing along with us, and we must've been talking too loudly because a nurse came in to pull the privacy curtain around us, blocking us off from the rest of the patients. And maybe the nurse would've chastised us, but she clearly liked to see the change in Richard.

But now we had some privacy, and it gave me an idea. I stood up and put my finger to my lips in a *shhhh* motion, then leaned over the bed, took Richard's face in my hands, and kissed him.

He was surprised at first, but after a second, he relaxed and kissed me back. It was all too brief but very sweet, and when I pulled away, his cheeks were scarlet-red. He glanced at Kat, chewed on his bottom lip, then burst out laughing. "I can't believe you did that," he said, his hand covering his mouth.

Kat leaned in and whispered like it was some big secret. "I think he's wanted to do that for a while."

"You don't mind?" he asked. "Seeing that?"

She patted him on the arm. "Not at all."

"Good," Richard whispered back to her. "Because I'd like him to do it again."

Now it was me who laughed. Not wanting to disappoint him, I lifted his chin with my finger and kissed him again.

We talked some more after that, about how he was being treated, and if he was allowed out of bed yet. "Nah. The doctors said I gotta stay like this for a few weeks yet, give myself some time to heal. He showed me the X-ray, and he said he never seen a bone break like fine china, so he fixed it with some kind of special metal plate and bolts. Said I should be as good as new in a few months."

"How long will you be here?" I asked. "All that time, or will they ship you somewhere else?"

"Somewhere else in the war?" he asked and I nodded. "Nope. My days in the army are done. Even if I wanted to go back for another tour, which I sure as hell don't, the doctor said there's no way I'd get medical clearance. I'm up for a medical discharge."

I sighed with relief, not really knowing how much I'd been dreading the thought of him going back to war until he said he wasn't. "Thank God," I breathed. "Thank God."

He gave me a sad smile. "There is no God in war. Not where I was anyway."

I took his hand and threaded our fingers. "You're home now. And when the doc says you're well enough to leave, you can come and stay with me."

"I'm guessing I'll be laid up here for months," he said. "Gotta have more surgeries yet."

"That's fine," I replied. "I can fly back every other weekend between now and then."

"It's too expensive!" Richard shook his head. "I can't let you do that."

"I have the money," I replied. Well, actually, my folks had the money, but that was beside the point. "Anyway, they have super cheap coach tickets. Just need to wait till the last minute, that's all. It's really no problem."

"You'd really do that for me?"

"Of course I would." I put his hand to my lips and kissed his knuckles. "There is nothing I wouldn't do for you."

He smiled, his cheeks tinting pink again. Then he put his fingertips to my beard, feeling the coarse whiskers. "I've missed this."

I gave my chin a scratch. "I was going to trim it back the other day."

"Or you could leave it," he said, blushing again.

"Or I could leave it," I said with a smile, kissing the palm of his hand.

We heard a nurse outside the curtain, so we pulled our hands apart. "When you come home with me, we'll have real privacy," I whispered.

He was chuckling when the nurse pulled back the curtain. If she noticed his flushed cheeks, she never mentioned it. "Ah, Mr. Ronsman, time for a quick checkup before lunch."

Lunchtime already? Wow, the time had gone so fast.

Kat pulled on my arm. "Richard, we'll be back when it's visiting hours again, okay?"

Richard craned his neck around the nurse to look at me. "You'll be back?"

"Of course."

He visibly relaxed, and the nurses distracted him with

the questions about all the gifts and the flowers he received today, telling him it was good to see him smile.

And when we came back in the afternoon, I brought him in a slice of apple pie. His eyes went wide and he grinned. "No way!"

"I remember you saying it was one of your favorites," I said. "They were serving it at the diner we found for lunch."

He ate that piece of pie like it was the best food he'd eaten in months. But the afternoon wore on, and as we talked about what we'd been doing at work and he told us a few more stories of his time in Vietnam—about the beautiful beaches and the village children who would laugh and play games—it was easy to see he was getting tired.

I doubted he'd spoken so much since he arrived back here.

His blinks were getting longer and he kept trying to shake it off. "You can sleep," I urged him.

"I don't want to miss a thing," he whispered.

"You won't. Kat and I have to get back to San Francisco soon anyway. And you have to write to me every day. I'll be back in a week or two, I promise. And we can speak on the phone." I took his hand, not caring who saw, and looked him right in the eyes. "You're not alone anymore."

He became teary. "Do you promise?"

I nodded. "With all my heart."

He closed his eyes and a tear slipped down his cheek, but he was soon asleep. We stayed there while he dozed. I saw other men resting, crying, yelling, babbling nonsense, resisting, and some were clearly sedated.

I was so very thankful that Richard was okay.

I knew it wasn't going to all be sunshine and roses. I'd seen the reports on television. Doctors saying the returned men suffered not just physically but mentally as well. More mentally than anything else. Depression, anxiety, bouts of anger. I knew what I was getting myself in for.

But as I watched him sleeping, I knew in my bones that he was worth it.

When the nurse tapped her watch signaling it was time for us to go, I needed to say goodbye. I didn't want him to wake up alone and wonder, again, if it had been a dream. I gently shook his arm. "Richard," I whispered.

His eyes flew open and he pulled back in fear, and I was sure if his leg had been better, he'd have jumped to his feet. He immediately winced and groaned in pain. He blinked a few times and let out an unsteady breath.

"Sorry," I said quickly. "I didn't mean to startle you."

He had a sheen of sweat across his brow and he'd paled considerably. He was panting shallow breaths. Kat called the nurse over and she came back a few seconds later with a white paper cup of pills. Richard took them quickly and he settled back in his bed.

After a moment, when my heart had returned to normal, I asked, "You okay?"

He nodded. "Yeah. I'm just a little jumpy until I get my bearings."

"I didn't mean to startle you," I said again. "I'm sorry. I didn't want you to wake up and for us to be gone."

He slow blinked. "You have to go already?"

I nodded. "I'll be back the weekend after next."

He frowned and I squeezed his hand. "I'm sorry. I fell asleep. I didn't want to," he whispered.

"It's fine. You need to rest. You have to write to me every day. I put our address and phone number on the inside of the notepad. I'm not losing you again."

He smiled, but it was chemically induced. "You're the best thing that's ever happened to me," he murmured.

"I'll see you again real soon. You concentrate on

getting better. San Francisco has a lot of hills, so we'll need your leg to heal the best it can, okay?" I squeezed his hand one last time. "And you can call me any time."

He let his head fall back, his eyes were glassy. Whatever drugs they'd given him worked well. He felt no pain now. "You really want a cripple?"

I leaned in and pressed my lips to the side of his head. "Don't talk about the man I love like that."

He grinned, and Kat leaned over and pressed a kiss to his cheek. "Take care, brother," she said with a wink. She pulled his dinner over for him and took the lid off the plate. "We'll see you again soon."

As we were walking out, the nurse gave us a kind smile. "Thank you for visiting. It's the first time any of us have seen him smile."

I looked back at him. He was now holding the fork and attempting to eat at the pace of a sloth. I laughed and said, "If you want him to actually eat sometime today, he might need a little assistance."

Richard looked toward us and laughed. "Love you," he said with a dopey grin.

Everyone in the room simply assumed he'd said it to Kat. She giggled and waved, but she knew, just like I did. He said it to me.

VISITS

July 28, 1970

THERE WERE no tears this time when I saw him, only ear-to-ear grins. The two weeks since I'd seen him dragged by. I spoke to him on the phone twice; he called me on my birthday and we spoke for so long the nurses had to ask him three times to end the call. I got two letters in the mail, sent one back, and delivered the second one by hand. He had another operation on his leg, and doctors thought that might be the last one. Now he just had more healing to do. He was so happy to see us. Kat came back with me, though she explained to the nursing staff that she had appointments downtown and it would only be me, Richard's brother-in-law, who would visit the next day.

I spent the whole time by his bedside. I brought him books, more soda, a T-shirt or two, and some more cookies and candy. And I also gave him some brochures on San Francisco, listing all the things to do and all the places to see.

He wanted to know every little detail about our apartment and about my job. I mentioned that he'd put on a much-needed pound or two, and when I told him he looked much better, his reply was simple. "Because now I have something to look forward to."

August 11, 1970

RICHARD HAD STARTED PHYSICAL THERAPY, and I could see the strain it had put on him. He was tired, his leg hurt, but somehow he still looked better. He was still confined to his bed. The physical therapist simply drew the privacy curtain around his bed and made him exercise his good leg and his arms right then and there in his bed.

His injured leg was still bandaged, and he was still thin. The war had certainly taken a toll on his body. He was embarrassed to have to do this in front of me, but when the therapists left, I told him it was a good thing. "So I can help you when you come home," I said.

He smiled and shook his head. "You're crazy."

I nodded. "For you."

The army had finally tracked down his backpack from Vietnam and his personal effects were forwarded onto him. Every single letter I'd written, the photos, and comic books were bundled up and shipped to him. He didn't want to go through them just yet, which was fine. The memories and heartbreak were just far too much.

"I need your help with something," he said.

"Anything."

"I want to write to Karel's girl." He swallowed hard. "I want her to know what kind of man he was, and how brave he was, and how he saved my life."

Oh, man.

"Yes, of course."

"I can ask one of the officers here to help track down an address, but if you could mail it for me…"

"It'd be my pleasure."

So I sat beside him as he penned it, and I held his hand as he sobbed.

August 25, 1970

RICHARD HAD PUT on another pound or two, and he looked healthier and stronger. Kat came back with me this time, and she couldn't believe the difference in him. He'd had a haircut and was clean-shaven, wearing one of his new shirts.

But the guys in the bed next to him and across from him were new, fresh from Vietnam. One lay on his side, and when he wasn't sedated, he was crying. And the other guy had lost one leg from the knee down and was in an awful lot of pain.

Every time he yelled or cried out, you could see it physically weigh on him, and not just on Richard, but on every man in the ward.

"Rico went home last week," Richard whispered. "Jimmy here—" He nodded to the man who lost his leg. "—he was only there for a month before they came under enemy fire. In with my old company, the fifth battalion. Said they lost a whole platoon. I don't know who's left."

He got that far away look in his eyes and his breathing

was shallow. I squeezed his hand, and he squeezed mine right back.

September 8, 1970

AS SOON AS I walked through the door, Richard grinned at me, more than just his happy-to-see-me smile. "What's up?"

A nurse had followed me in, pushing a wheelchair. "Your chariot," she said with a smile.

Richard threw back the bedsheet, and I dashed to his side. "Whoa, slow down," I said, taking his arm.

His left leg was still bandaged from hip to knee, and the nurse and I helped him stand first, then slowly lowered him into the wheelchair. His left leg stuck straight out, and the nurse fixed some prop for it at the base. We put a blanket over his lap, I grabbed the bag I brought with me, and I wheeled him out of the ward. "You never told me you had a chair," I said as we made our way down the corridor.

"I wanted to surprise you. This is only my second time."

"Where did you want to go?"

"San Francisco."

I laughed. "No, I mean where am I pushing you to?"

"There's a courtyard down here on the right. I need to feel the sun."

As soon as we pushed through the doors and went into the fresh air and the sunshine, Richard put his head back and closed his eyes. "Oh my God. It's been ten weeks since I've been outside. That feels *so* good."

I pushed him to the far end of the yard. There was a tree for shade and a seat for me. And there we sat for hours. I showed him all the new things I bought for him, including some fruit and sodas, which meant we didn't have to leave the courtyard.

"It is so good to be outside here with you," he said. "No one listening in, no nurses interrupting. This is like heaven."

"Just imagine," I replied. "When you come home, we get to have this every day. I can bring you coffee in bed before I go to work, and we can have dinner by candlelight every night if we want."

"Sounds perfect."

"Have the doctors told you how long…?"

He shook his head. "Not yet."

"Have your parents called?"

He frowned. "My mom called last week. Said they've been busy with the late harvest. Too busy to visit, maybe. But she's only called three times the entire time I've been here. If they say actions speak louder than words, then I can hear their message loud and clear. Guess they kind of struck out when they got me as a son."

I took his hand. "Fuck them. You're the opposite of a disappointment. If they can't see you for the man you are, for the beautiful person you are, then fuck them. You, me, Kat, and my folks, we'll be the only family you'll ever need."

September 22, 1970

RICHARD WAS EXHAUSTED. The physical therapist had him on his feet walking between two railings every day for the last week. After being bedridden for almost three months, it was a huge strain on his body.

It was hard to watch. But he knew he had to go through this to get better. He struggled, almost fell once, and his determination was nothing short of fierce. I could see why he made a good soldier, why he got promoted and was a squad leader. Because he didn't know how to quit.

And when he got to the end of the railing by himself, his physical therapist cheered, and I was so proud I damn near cried.

October 6, 1970

WHEN I ARRIVED, I just walked through like I always did but stopped cold when I saw his bed had been stripped. "Where is he?" I asked the closest nurse.

Her face fell. "Is his sister not here?"

"Uh, no. She has a head cold and didn't want to share it with anyone. I'm sorry, but you're scaring me. Where is he? Is he okay?"

"He has an infection. Come with me."

I was given a mask and taken to a room where he was. It was a private room, isolated even, and he was on the bed with tubes and machines and… "Oh my God," I whispered. "Is he going to be okay?"

"He has a blood infection. Started in his wound area and spread, and it's affecting his lungs. We caught it early, though he's on some strong medications that keep him sedated."

She didn't answer my question, so I asked it again. "Is he going to be okay?"

"We can't make any promises, sir. But it lifts his spirits when you're here, so it's a good thing you arrived today."

She gave me a smile. "The next forty-eight hours will be telling."

I put the mask on, she opened the door for me, and I stepped inside. My feet felt like lead. I sat beside him with my back to the door and took his hand. He didn't clasp my fingers like he normally did, and I hung my head and cried. He'd come so far. We were so close.

"I'm not giving up," I said, not knowing if he could hear me or not. Then I watched him sleep and listened to him breathe until the nurse told me I had to leave.

THE NEXT MORNING, I arrived at just before nine and as soon as the nurse saw me, she smiled. "Good news," she said as she walked me to his room. "His temperature is down, respiratory is improving, and his blood counts were better, which is all a good sign."

"Is he awake?"

She nodded toward the door. "Go in and see."

I stepped inside, and when Richard turned his head to look at whoever entered and saw it was me, he gave me a tired, slow smile.

"Hey," I said quietly. I was quick to sit beside him and take his hand. "You're awake!"

He slow blinked. "I feel like I've been hit by a truck."

"You were quite sick," I told him.

"Doc said I'm lucky," he murmured. "Don't feel it right now."

"You're a fighter," I told him. "The bravest man I know."

He smiled and closed his eyes. "Will you stay a while."

I lifted his hand and kissed his knuckles. "As long as I'm

allowed. I brought that book you talked about. I could read it for you if you like?"

He didn't open his eyes, but he was still smiling. "I would like that very much."

I took my copy of *The Andromeda Strain* out of my bag, turned to page one, and began to read it out loud.

October 20, 1970

I'D SPOKEN to him during the week and I'd written twice, knowing receiving mail was a welcome break in the monotony of his hospital stay.

He was still on strong antibiotics and pain meds, and he was exhausted, but he was getting better every day. It was a setback, but the doctor said he was expected to make a full recovery.

He was frustrated and disappointed. I couldn't blame him. I wanted him to come home too, but I could see the bigger picture. "I don't care how long it takes," I whispered to him so no one else could hear. "As long as you're alive and healthy, I can wait."

"Are you sure you don't want to… find someone else?" he asked. His bottom lip trembled as though he was fighting tears. "Someone who isn't stuck in here. Someone who isn't a cripple."

"It's a bit hard to find someone else when I only have eyes for you," I replied. I took his hand and uncurled his fingers. "I get you're angry and frustrated, and I don't blame you. You're allowed to be. But I don't want anyone else. And I've told you before, not to call the man I love a cripple."

He sulked for all of five seconds. "How can I stay mad at you?"

I laughed. "You can't. Because Kat came with me this trip. She just had to run to the mall for a few last-minute things, and we brought enough candy with us for everyone in your ward. We thought you could celebrate Halloween early."

He was allowed to use a wheelchair for a short time, so on Sunday we wheeled around his ward, trick or treating. Not everyone was up for it, but most of the men smiled. Maybe it was because Kat dressed up as a sexy witch, and Richard had to tell a few guys not to ogle his sister a couple of times.

When we left on Sunday afternoon, Richard was tired, but he hadn't stopped smiling yet.

November 24, 1970

RICHARD WAS GETTING STEADILY STRONGER, though it was slow, it was definitely progress. He was getting back into physical therapy in the last week, albeit slower after his blood infection. It was a positive step forward, and his sole motivation was that the harder he focused, the sooner he could go home.

We planned a special Thanksgiving lunch. We were allowed to sit on a picnic blanket out in the sunny courtyard. Richard had blankets over him because the wind was cool, but the sunshine was too good to miss.

He lay on his back, alongside me and Kat, and we pointed out shapes in the clouds until it became too cool for Richard. I helped him into his chair and Kat put the blanket over his lap and made sure his leg was okay.

"Before we go inside," he said. "I just want to say thank you. For everything. You have no idea how much it means. Gary, and you too, Kat. If it weren't for you both, well I… I don't know if I would've survived this."

I crouched down at his side and took his hand. "You're stronger than you know."

"I'm stronger because of you, Gary. I'm alive because of you. When I was in Vietnam, it was the thought of you that kept me alive. I had something to come home for. And when I was injured and I was shipped out without any of my letters and I had no way of contacting you, I was lost, ya know? Like every day was dark and a blur. And then you found me again." He swallowed hard and let out a shaky breath. "If you hadn't, I would have drowned myself in every bottle, in any drug I could find. I knew I would. Like most guys who leave here. But now I have a new purpose. And even if you didn't want me, I'd still be grateful because you got me through the darkest days of my life."

"If I didn't want you?" I asked. "Never gonna happen." He smiled and his cheeks tinted pink. "You are loved, Richard."

His hold on my hand tightened. "And so are you."

Kat sniffled beside us and we both looked up at her. "Are you two done ruining every man for me? How will I ever find someone who says such sappy things to me?"

Richard laughed and took her hand. "You're loved too."

She rolled her eyes. "Yeah, yeah. No need to rub it in," she said, but she was smiling. "Just so you know, you're on dinner duty when you move in."

"Deal," Richard said with a laugh. "I hope you like toast."

December 6, 1970

I COULD HEAR the ringing phone as I was trying to get my key in the door when I got home from work. I dashed for it. "Hello?"

"Gary," Richard said.

His familiar voice made me smile. "This is a nice surprise." I'd only spoken to him two days before. "What's up?"

"I was just calling to see if you've booked a plane ticket for this weekend."

"No, I haven't yet. I was going to call the airline tomorrow, get a cheaper deal."

"Well, I was going to ask you not to come this weekend."

My heart dropped. "Why?"

"Because I have a date."

A what?

My mind sped up but couldn't find traction. "A what? Richard, what are you saying? What do you mean?"

His laughter sounded down the line. "Not that kind of

date, silly. A date to leave. The doc gave me a date to leave."

"A what?" Instant tears burned in my eyes and my heart swelled. "What?"

"I can leave the hospital."

I almost fell into a chair at the table. "When?"

"The last three days, I walked the length of the ward with a cane, and the doc said if I can do it every day for a week, he'll sign my release."

"Can you do it?"

He scoffed. "You watch me."

I could barely speak. "A week?"

"You okay?" he asked gently.

"I'm crying," I said, though I didn't know why. It was pretty obvious.

"Oh, don't cry," he cooed. "It's good news. Isn't it?"

"It's the best news," I said, wiping my face. "You'll be home for Christmas."

"I've got money for a plane ticket, but I don't have much money for any gifts," he said quietly. "So I don't know how special Christmas will be."

"Are you kidding? It'll be the best Christmas ever." I shook off my tears. "I made you a promise last year, remember? When you were in Vietnam and it was your first Christmas away from home. I promised you this year I'd make it a special Christmas. There's no wood fire here, but we don't need money, baby. We'll be together, and that's all we need."

He let out a shaky breath. "So, will you meet me at the airport?"

"No. I wanna be there when you walk out of the hospital. I'll be there every step of the way."

"You sure?"

"Every step of the way, baby. Every step."

CHAPTER EIGHT

RICHARD

WHEN GARY WALKED into the hospital ward, I was dressed and ready to go. My wound was dressed, my bag was packed, and I was dying to leave. I met him at the end of my bed, using a walking cane that was now mine.

"Look at you," he whispered.

It took every ounce of willpower not to throw my arms around him right there in front of everyone. I wanted to kiss him for hours. I wanted to do all sorts of things to him, but mostly, I wanted to be in his arms.

But first I had to leave the hospital and leave my life in the army behind me. I was so ready for the horrors of the last year to be over, and for the next part of my life to begin. "Civilian clothes," I said, holding my free hand out to the side. "It's been a while."

He grinned. "You ready?"

"I am so ready."

He grabbed my duffle bag off the bed and I said goodbye to the guys on the ward, then I said goodbye to the nurses and the doctors on my way out, shook hands, kissed cheeks, waved them all off. They wanted me to leave in a wheelchair, but there was no way—no freaking way—I wasn't walking out of there. It was more of a hobble, and it was slow and cautious, but I was damn well walking out.

I got to the front doors of the hospital and walked out into the sunshine. I stopped, stood there for a moment, and closed my eyes to the feel of the warmth on my face. Even in winter, the rays of sunshine were like heaven. When I opened my eyes again, Gary was watching me. "You good?" he asked, smiling.

"It's like the first day of the rest of my life," I answered. "No more war, no more hospital, no more hospital food."

"And you can finally start living the life you were meant to live," he said. "Your true life. Where you can be the real you."

I nodded and blinked back tears. "I promised myself I wouldn't cry today."

He laughed. "Deal. No crying." He hailed a cab, and once we were both in the back seat, he fussed over my leg, asking if I was okay, if it hurt, did I need to sit in the front where there was more room. All I could do was shake my head. I let my pinkie rest against his on the seat between us where the driver couldn't see. "Here is fine," I said. There was no place else I wanted to be but right next to him.

"Where to?" the driver asked.

"Lindbergh airport," Gary said. "But if you could go past a few tourist spots and a burger joint before we get to the airport, that'd be great. Richard here has been laid up in the hospital for months and hasn't seen any of San Diego, so I'd like him to see the sights, if that's okay."

The driver nodded, and he took us to Coronado Beach, then through the Gaslamp district, then to a burger place called Hodad's at the end of Santa Monica Avenue at Ocean Beach. Gary bought the driver a burger, so he stopped the meter while we ate. I'd never tasted food so good.

By the time we got to the airport, I had a belly full of food and was dog-tired. Walking through the airport was hard enough, but there were steps and narrow aisles on the plane I had to maneuver, and after getting in and out of the cab and all this walking, my leg was killing me. I tried not to let on, but Gary knew. "Have you got your pills?" he asked.

"They're in my bag," I replied. We'd checked my bag in at the check-in already. "I'll be okay."

He was worried but thankfully didn't push. "Well, just let me know if it gets worse," was all he said.

I gave him the best smile I could manage. "I just can't wait to get home… Well, to your home. It's a bit weird for me to call it that considering I've never been there."

"You'll love it. The apartment isn't anything fancy," he said. Then he leaned in and whispered in my ear, "But it's private."

I felt my face flame and warmth spread straight to my groin, making me shift in my seat.

"Are you okay?" he asked, worried about my leg.

I cleared my throat. "It's not my leg."

It took him half a second to catch on and he laughed. "Not long to wait now," he said.

The stewardess interrupted with a much-needed distraction as the plane taxied out. But I was asleep, my head resting on Gary's shoulder before we made altitude.

GARY MIGHT HAVE THOUGHT the apartment wasn't anything fancy, but to me, it might as well have been the Hilton. I could have done without the single flight of stairs to get to it, but inside was clean, bright, and warm. There was a living room with brown carpet and white-and-orange curtains. There were two loveseats and a walnut console television. Gary noticed me staring at it. "Kat got it secondhand when we moved here. It's a few years old, but it's color and it works," he said as he put my duffle bag on the sofa.

"My mom and dad have one just like it," I said.

Gary frowned at that. "Did you want to call them?"

"Maybe tomorrow," I replied.

"Okay. No rush." Then he showed me the kitchen. The cabinets were oak. The counters were laminated orange. The linoleum floor was brown. The oven and fridge looked a little old but clean, functional.

"What do you think?" Gary asked.

"It's perfect," I said. "I've only ever lived with my parents or in a war zone or a hospital, so this is crazy cool."

He grinned, then led me to the hall. "Bathroom here, and Kat's bedroom, and… our bedroom." He pushed open the door and stood aside. "No pressure. If you'd rather me take the couch for a bit, or whatever, you just need to say. I don't want you to think you don't have options."

I stepped into the room. It was simple: a double bed, a small table at one side—Gary's side of the bed. There stood a lamp, an alarm clock, and a book. There was a dresser and a chest of drawers. The shag carpet was brown, the wallpaper cream, and the curtains were the same as in the living room. The bedspread was blue.

The bed.

Suddenly my pulse took off and my pants grew a little tight. We were finally alone. It had been far too long.

"Where's Kat?" I asked.

"She's at work." He looked at his watch. "She won't be home until after five. So, two hours away. She was so excited for you to come home today."

I could feel my cheeks heat with anticipation, with the mere thought of being alone with him. "So we're alone?"

Gary, still standing at the doorway, clued in, and his smile pulled at one side of his lips. "We are. Is there anything you'd like to do while we're alone?" Now he smirked.

"Plenty." I swallowed hard. "I don't know what my leg will let me do, but I reckon if you don't come over here and touch me, I think I might pass out."

He took a few slow and deliberate steps. "Just touching?"

"Touching, kissing, holding," I whispered. "I need to feel you."

He gently cupped my face and I immediately leaned into his hand. He put his thumb to my bottom lip and opened my mouth, so tenderly, before he crushed his lips to mine. He slid both his arms around me and held me, pulling me against him, holding me up, and he devoured me with his kiss. I dropped my cane and threw my arms around his neck, and we stood there and kissed until we needed air.

Then, still holding me, he walked me to the bed and laid me down. He made sure my leg was okay and I wasn't in any pain, and he was fussing. "Do you want a pillow under your knee?"

"What are you doing?" I asked. "Gary, my leg isn't my biggest concern right now."

Smiling, he finally lay down next to me, his nose brushing mine. "I don't want to hurt you."

"Then hold me. And kiss me," I whispered. "Because if you don't, I don't know what—"

He cut my words off with his mouth, filling mine with his tongue while his arms gently pulled me close. We were on our sides now, my left leg on top. His arm was under my head, and our bodies melded together. The feel of his erection against mine almost did me in.

"It's been so long," I panted when we broke for air.

"For me too," he replied. "Can I make you come?"

I shivered at his words. "God, yes, please."

He popped my button fly and slid his hands down over my briefs, being careful of my leg. "Is that okay?"

"So good." But the truth was, I couldn't feel anything but his hand on my dick. I thrust against his palm and he gripped me, then crushed his mouth to mine once more, and just a few short strokes later, I came. I groaned as the pleasure only he could draw from me took me over the edge. I came all over his hand, between us, over us.

"Holy shit," he mumbled, then quickly undid his own jeans. It took me a few brain-hazy moments to catch on, but I wrapped my hand around his length, relishing in the feel of him. Hot and hard and skin on skin, and he fucked my fist and trembled as he came.

After a year of hell, death, and pain, it was such a beautiful thing to witness, to be a part of.

As the high of my orgasm subsided, the ache in my leg came back. Gary grabbed my bag from the living room and handed me my pills and a glass of water. Then he came back with a warm, wet washcloth and cleaned us both up before he climbed back onto the bed, pulled me against him so my head was on his chest, and he held me until I fell asleep.

I was exhausted. The traveling, the walking, then sex was more than my body was used to. And he was one hundred percent warmth and comfort and safety, and he was my home. I felt like I'd spent my whole life adrift, like a bird with no nest, no branch to rest upon. Always in flight, too afraid to land.

Well, I'd just landed for the first time in my life. And I dozed in that half-awake, half-asleep state, tired but too overwhelmed to sleep. I didn't want to miss a thing. I wanted to hold him, be close to him, touch him. I was now living with a man. A man whom I loved, who kept me sane when I was immersed in madness. A man who gave me hope when I had none.

"I love you, Gary," I whispered.

He hummed contentedly and kissed my forehead, my cheek, my lips. "And I love you."

"I'm finally here," I mumbled.

"Where you belong."

I couldn't keep my eyes open and I could barely form words. "It doesn't feel real. Like it's too good to be true. Like if I fall asleep, I'll wake up and it will have been a dream."

He tightened his hold on me and kissed my temple. "Don't fight sleep, baby," he whispered. "I promise it's not a dream."

"Pretty sure your beard wouldn't tickle me in a dream."

He chuckled, and the sound reverberated against my ear. Then he rubbed circles on my back, and he stroked my hair, nuzzled into me, and I was lost to it.

Sleep. Him. Love.

All of it.

I WOKE up and it took me a few seconds to get my bearings. I wasn't in Vietnam. I wasn't in the hospital. The bed was soft and warm, and Gary's coat hung over the door…

His alarm clock, his book. His dresser, his smell. And I remembered; I was at Gary's. I was safe and loved, and it made me smile.

Then I caught traces of something else. The smell of something cooking and soft voices coming from somewhere. I got myself up, and I noticed my walking cane propped against the bedside table. Gary must've thought to put it there.

That made me smile too.

I made myself as presentable as I could, followed my nose and found Gary and Kat in the kitchen. "Here he is!" Gary said, his face lighting up.

Kat was quick to give me a hug. "Oh my God, you're finally here! It's so good to see you out of the hospital. Gary's been counting down like a kid waiting for Christmas."

My face heated as embarrassment tinted my cheeks. "It's good to be here," I said. "Finally."

"Well, you look great," Kat said.

I held up the walking cane and gave a bit of a shrug. "I'll have this for a while. Probably forever."

"As long as you're here, that's all that matters," Gary said, sliding his arm around my waist. It felt strange that we were free to do that, to be affectionate with one another, especially in front of other people. I knew it would take some getting used to.

Being together at Woodstock was different. That was like three days away from reality, away from the church and the government, who were opposed to people like us. But in the real world, it was still against the law to be homosexual, and although views and public perception were changing, the law was the law.

But in the privacy of this apartment, we were free to be

our true selves. So when Gary put his arm around me, I leaned against him, relishing in the contact.

"Something smells great," I said. "I didn't mean to fall asleep. I thought I was on dinner duty."

Kat laughed. "We'll give you a day to get settled." Then she checked the oven. "Gary made dinner tonight. Home-cooked casserole."

I turned to him. "You cooked it?"

"Don't look so surprised," he said with a smile. "It's my mom's recipe. Not as good as the one she makes, but I wanted to do something special for your first night here. Home cooking and not hospital food."

"Thank you. That means a lot," I murmured into his chest. He was quick to rub my back and kiss the side of my head, which might have been such a small gesture to someone else, but to me, it meant the world.

Kat gave us a fond smile. "Well, it smells delicious."

"It's almost done," he said. Then he pulled back so he could ask me, "Are you hungry?"

"Starving."

A short time later, we had the table set and dinner served. I was a little slow, with my leg and all, but they were very patient and nothing was a problem. Kat asked us about our day and our flight from San Diego, Gary asked her about her day at work, and it was crazy how grown-up I felt. Sitting at the dining table having dinner and an adult conversation. I couldn't help but marvel at how normal it was and how ridiculously wonderful that felt.

There was no talk about my parents' farm, crops, or the weather. There were no discussions on my father's church and how if I were a normal son, I would've found a wife by now. There was no talk of the war, of who was injured, and who wasn't coming home.

"How does that sound?" Gary asked. "Richard?"

I blinked back to my senses. "I'm sorry, I was a million miles away. What was the question?"

"I was just telling Kat I thought on the weekend we might be able to go out and get a Christmas tree. There's a guy selling them from an empty lot two blocks over. Just a small tree, and we can decorate it and start to make the place feel special."

"Oh, sure, that sounds great," I replied. "I'd really like that."

"I have to go to work tomorrow," Gary said.

I couldn't keep the disappointment from my voice. "You do?"

He nodded. "And the day after, but then it's the week-end. I kinda figured you could do with two days' rest and maybe a few short walks to get your bearings."

"True," I conceded.

"But?" Gary prodded, reading me far too easily.

"But he's gonna miss you," Kat answered for me.

I laughed but felt my face go bright red. "I wasn't going to say that."

Gary chuckled, leaned over, and kissed my cheek, causing my blush to deepen. "Dinner's really good, by the way," I said, hoping to change the subject.

"I'll miss you too," he said.

I grinned at him, even though I was embarrassed, and Kat groaned. "Oh, you guys are going to kill me with lovey-dovey stuff." There was no bite in her tone. She looked at us affectionately. "I'm really happy you're here, Richard. Not as happy as Gary is, but still happy." She winked at me.

"I am too," I answered. "More than I can say."

There was something I needed to tell them both, and I figured my first day here was the best time to do it. "If it weren't for you both, I don't know where I would've ended up. And I have a little money, and I'll get my pension, which isn't much. But I want you both to know I'll look for work as soon as I'm able. I won't be a burden, I promise."

Gary took my hand. "You could never be a burden."

"Richard," Kat added. "We would never think of you like that. It won't be easy, and we understand that."

I gave her a quick smile but I avoided Gary's eyes. "Hey," he said, and I eventually looked at him. "You're not a burden," he repeated. "And what have I told you about speaking about the man I love like that?"

My heart banged against my ribs and my face burned so hot I thought it might catch fire. Gary laughed and scooted his chair closer so he could pull me against his chest. "I love the way he blushes."

I hid my face in his neck. "You're embarrassing me."

He lifted my chin and kissed me right on the lips in front of Kat. "You better get used to me telling you how awesome you are."

I bit my lip and glanced at Kat. "Sorry."

Kat stood up. "I'll do the dishes," she said. I started to object—it was only right that I did them given I wasn't paying rent—but she raised her hand to stop me. "This is a one-time offer," she said with a smile. "It's your first night here and I'm pretty sure Gary has other plans for you, more private plans, given he's waited over a year for you to get here."

Oh my God. She was implying she should clean up so Gary and I could be… sexual. My mouth fell open and Gary laughed. He pushed his chair out and helped me to my feet. He handed me my walking cane. "We better not disappoint her."

Kat collected the plates and laughed as she walked into the kitchen. "Thank you for dinner, Gary," she called out.

"You're welcome, Kat," he replied. Then, still grinning,

he leaned and kissed me. "I do have more private plans, if that's okay with you?" he murmured in a voice that went straight to my groin.

I nodded and he kissed me, making me feel warm all over. Then he took my hand and led me to his room.

Our room.

I didn't have time to think about what that meant, because as soon as he'd closed the door behind us, he was undressing me.

CHAPTER NINE

GARY

RICHARD WAS A PARADOX, that was for sure. He'd lived through hell, survived the jungles of Vietnam, being shot at, getting injured. He'd watched people die. He'd lost his best friend over there. Yet he could still blush like that innocent farm boy I'd met last year on our way to Woodstock.

But he was right when he said he had changed. It wasn't a bad change; it was just that the wide-eyed, innocent shine to his eyes had dulled a little. I guessed war did that. I'd heard a lot about the returned soldiers who had severe psychological issues. But still, society scorned the Vietnam veterans. It was horrible. Richard had suffered indescribable horrors over there and now returned to have his own country hate him for it.

I would try and protect him from that ugliness all I could, and if cocooning him in the apartment and surrounding him with love was all I could do, then I would damn well do it.

On that first night, after Kat had rendered him speechless with embarrassment, I'd taken him to our room and began to undress him. Slowly revealing each sliver of skin and planting kisses on his chest, his collarbone, his shoulder, his belly. Then I took extra care taking off his pants, paying particular attention to his bandaged leg. I ignored his cock for now, kissing his hip, his thigh, the inner calf of his good leg. Then I took the foot on his injured leg and kissed the top of his foot, his shin, his knee.

He was on the bed, his cock hard and lying across to his hip. I crawled up his legs until I could lick his length and take in his scent. "Remember at Woodstock, you told me you wanted to try everything?"

His head was propped up on a few pillows, his fingers found my hair, and he nodded. "Yeah."

"Well, I want to show you everything. I want you to experience everything, feel everything." I nudged his cock with my nose, licked his balls, and made him hiss. "I want to cherish every part of your body, show you how much you mean to me."

He writhed under me, rolling his hips in search of friction. "I dreamed of this," he whispered. "Of everything you'd do to me. Since the day I left you standing by the road at Woodstock. All the ways you would make me yours."

"I don't want to rush you," I murmured, tonguing his shaft and sucking the head into my mouth, savoring his taste before pulling off. "But with your leg, we're going to need to take it slow."

He nodded, but he was so turned on, I was pretty sure he'd agree to anything. I undid my jeans and kissed up his stomach, his chest, his neck and jaw, finally finding his mouth. I put my weight on him, careful of his leg, and he was grinding against me. Leaning up on one hand, I took my erection out of my briefs and held both our cocks in my hand. Sliding our shafts together, fucking my fist. His eyes were wide, like he'd never seen such a thing done before, and he began to thrust harder and whimper. I crushed my lips against his, plowing my tongue into his mouth, and it was too much for him. He came with a strangled cry, shooting streams of come onto his stomach. The way he pulsed in my hand, against my own cock, brought me undone and I followed quickly after.

We lay there in each other's arms, me holding him and him holding me. "I can't believe this is real," he murmured. "That this is my life."

"It's not some acid trip like you had at Woodstock. There are no fluffy bunnies here."

He froze, then laughed. "Oh my God, I'd forgotten all about that."

"I haven't," I admitted. "Watching you dance in the rain by yourself without a care in the world… I think I fell in love with you right there."

He pulled back to look me in the eye. "You did?"

I nodded. "Yep. I thought, 'This man, this beautiful man has to be mine.'"

He snuggled back in. "I am. I am yours."

I tightened my hold on him. "I know. And I am yours."

After a moment, he said, "I fell in love with you the second I saw you in that diner."

I chuckled. "You told me that in a letter."

"It's the truth. You asked if you could sit down, and I looked up into the most handsome face I'd ever seen. With eyes I could get lost in, and the kindest smile." He was quiet a moment. "Or maybe it was when you made love to me that very first time. The way you moved inside me. I didn't know men could love that way. Or maybe it was when I got your first letter when I was overseas. Or every letter. I think I fell in love with you a little more every letter I got. But then there was that moment you walked into the hospital that first time and I'd almost given up hope, but you walked in, and the moment you saw me, I knew. I knew from the look on your face that there'd never be another man for me."

I pulled his face to mine and kissed him, trying to tell him what my words couldn't say. When the kiss slowed to a stop, I pulled him back into my arms. "I love you," I said. "And I am so glad you're here."

LEAVING him asleep in my bed the next morning to go to work was one of the hardest things I'd ever done. I could've easily stayed in bed with him, talking and laughing, making out and making love. But I'd already taken all the days off I could and we needed the money, so with a kiss to his forehead, I went to work.

I told myself the next two days when he would be at home by himself would be good for him. He could take a short walk and find his bearings in this new city. The apartment was kind of close to everything, and he could catch a bus or a tram to anywhere he needed. And letting him do it at his pace felt like the right thing to do.

I resisted calling home during the day, even though I thought of him a hundred times. But man, I was anxious to get home. Just knowing he was there waiting for me was the absolute highlight of my day.

I slid the key into the lock and pushed open the door, all but falling inside. He poked his head out from the kitchen, and seeing it was me, he walked out to greet me. He limped on his cane, but his smile was wide. "I'm so glad to see you," he said.

I took his face in my hands and kissed him. "Everything okay? How was your day?"

"It was fine," he replied. "I went for a walk to the end of the block. The sun was nice, and it felt great to get out."

"How was your leg?"

"It doesn't like the stairs much, but it was fine. I didn't realize how tired I would get, that's all. I'm sure if I do it every day I'll be able to get a little farther each time."

I kissed him again. "I'm proud of you."

That made him smile. "Thank you."

"Is that dinner I can smell?"

"Well it's supposed to be," he replied. "But it might need some help."

I laughed at that and we went into the kitchen. It was some kind of goulash and it smelled just fine, but he smelled better. I pushed him against the kitchen counter, careful of his leg, and pressed my body against his.

He was quick to respond, our mouths and our hands becoming desperate, fevered. I couldn't get enough of him. "When will Kat be home?" he asked breathily as I kissed down his neck.

"We've got about thirty minutes," I replied, fumbling with his button fly.

"We shouldn't do this here," he said, undoing my trousers. He slid his hand into my briefs and wrapped his fingers around me.

He was right. We shouldn't do this here. I pulled his hand out and, keeping hold of it, led him to our room. "Sit on the edge of the bed," I ordered. He limped over to it and sat, keeping his left leg out straight. I walked over and stood in front of him. "Is your leg okay?"

He nodded, looking up at me with his kiss-swollen lips and darkened eyes.

Then I freed my hard cock. "Good." I put my thumb to his bottom lip. "Open wide."

He licked his lips and smiled.

THE NEXT DAY was much the same. I had to go to work and Richard had plans to find the closest VA office and make sure his paperwork was all up to date. I asked if he wanted me to go with him, given how the protests were still going on, but he was adamant. I left my work phone number with him in case he needed it, kissed him goodbye, and went to work.

I was anxious all day, and I raced home from the bus. "Richard?" I called out as I came to the door. "Richard?"

He walked out from the hall, limping on his cane. "What's wrong?"

Relief flooded through me the moment I saw him. I put my hands on his shoulders. "Are you okay?"

"Yes, why wouldn't I be?"

"I've been worried about you all day," I replied, pulling him in for a hug.

"Worried about what? It was just paperwork. A change of address, that's all."

I laughed with relief. "No protesters?"

He shook his head. "Nope. But I'm making chili for dinner. I think it could use some more flavor."

I laughed again, kissed him soundly on the lips, and went into the kitchen to save dinner.

We spent the night on the couch watching television: Kat on one sofa, Richard and me on the other. It was so normal and boring, and utterly perfect.

"What are your plans for tomorrow?" Kat asked during a commercial.

"We're going Christmas tree shopping," I answered. I didn't even try to hide how excited I was. "We're gonna get a tree and decorations. Maybe even a gift or two."

Richard sat with his back against my chest and I

hooked my arm over his shoulder. "Just how much walking is involved tomorrow?"

I laughed. "Not much." I also knew he was worried about spending money. He'd said before he didn't have much money for Christmas. "The tree lot is just two blocks over, and there's a huge thrift store close by."

"Oh," Kat said. "I need a new coat."

"You should come with us," Richard said. Then he looked at me and cringed. "Sorry. I should have asked if that was okay with you first."

I gave him a squeeze. "That's a great idea. The three of us should go. We can choose the tree, pick out decorations, and buy a small gift or two from the store. It'll be perfect." Kat was happy with that, and Richard smiled. He relaxed back against me and I gave him a gentle squeeze. "We can get a whole bunch of stuff to make the apartment look all Christmassy. It doesn't have to cost us a fortune. We'll check out the thrift store and see what we can put together."

"You're really excited about it, aren't you?" Kat asked.

I nodded and kissed the side of Richard's head. "I made a promise, and I intend to keep it."

WINTER IN SAN FRANCISCO was nowhere near as cold as back home. There was no snow for one thing, which would make Christmas different for us, but I was grateful because it meant Richard could walk on the sidewalks without worrying too much about slipping or sliding—or worse, falling—with his injured leg.

We walked at his pace to the tree lot and picked out a small but healthy-looking tree that would fit in our apartment. "You guys head to the thrift store, and I'll run the tree back home so we don't have to carry it everywhere. It'll give you both time to buy me something small, because I'm totally not opposed to surprise Christmas gifts."

Richard laughed and Kat linked her arm through his and they walked toward the thrift store while I lugged the small tree back to the apartment. I also wanted them to have some time to talk without me being around, and this was the perfect opportunity. I wanted them to become friends. More for Richard's sake than Kat's. I mean, I wanted her to like him, which she already did. But his social circles were nonexistent right now, and if anyone could help him make friends, it was Kat.

People were also less suspicious of Kat and Richard together than they were of Richard and me together. Sure, times were changing and San Francisco and California were open-minded places, but being gay was still frowned upon by most, and it was, above everything else, against the law.

By the time I got back to the thrift store, I found them toward the rear. It was a large store with quite a few rows of clothes and household items. Kat was trying on scarves and coats and Richard was laughing at something she'd said. The sight and sound of that were almost worth the splinters and stitch in my side from hurriedly taking the tree back by myself.

"Oh, Gary," Kat said. She spotted me first. "What do you think of this one?" She pulled the scarf from around her neck. It was purple and orange and kinda gaudy but also kinda cool.

"It'd match your purple coat," I said. I walked down the aisle she was in, across a row of waist-high shelves of scarves and hats, to where Richard stood on the other side.

"And my orange shoes!" she said, cheerfully.

"I told her she should get it," Richard said with a smile.

"Did you find anything?" I asked him.

"Nothing yet. This place is huge." He looked down the aisle. "I don't even know where to start."

"What did you need?" I asked him.

"A coat." He shrugged. "Maybe some slacks and some sweatpants. I have those two shirts you bought me, so maybe a sweater."

I could tell he felt a little bad. He'd basically moved in with nothing, and here he was shopping in a secondhand store, so I wanted to make this fun. I held up coat after coat, sweater after sweater, and slacks, pants, and sweats, making jokes and trying and succeeding in making him laugh.

It was my most favorite sound.

Aside from the sounds he made in bed, that is, but his laughter truly made my heart happy.

Once we'd found him a few new things to wear, we began on the Christmas decorations. We found tinsel and baubles, tree ornaments, and a tablecloth with snowmen on it. There was even a small plastic tree for a centerpiece.

But as we shopped and spent time rummaging through discount bins near the service counter, I noticed Richard shifting his weight off his bad leg and leaning a little.

"We're almost done," I said. "But here, take a seat." There were two seats beside the service counter, which I assumed were for staff during quiet times.

The small older lady behind the counter came over. "Yes, take a seat, dear," she said. She had long gray hair pulled up in a twist, wore an apron, and she looked frail, though I didn't doubt she worked fourteen-hour days. She had a kind face and helped Richard into the seat, which he took gratefully.

I left him in her good company while I found three

stockings to hang up, and while Richard was distracted, I murmured to Kat, "Help! I need to find him something."

"He looked at that a few times," she whispered, nodding toward the shelves of knick-knacks. "The wooden cigar box."

"He did?"

"Yep. Opened, looked it over. Checked the price and put it back." She picked up some reindeer figurines and pretended to inspect them. "But his eyes kept going back to it."

I had no idea what he would want the box for, but it sounded as if he clearly liked it. I looked over to where Richard was sitting, and when I saw he was chatting with the sales lady, I snuck over and grabbed the box. There were two silver photo frames alongside it, so I picked them up as well. I went back to where Kat was now inspecting some garlands and stashed the box and the photo frames in among all the Christmas decorations. "When we leave," I said. "I'll pretend I've forgotten something and come back and get them."

"Good idea." She took her collection over to the sales counter and smiled at Richard. "Did you want anything else?"

"No thank you," he said politely. He got to his feet, leaning heavily on his cane, and he limped over to us."

"You okay?" I asked, dumping my shopping on the counter so I could look at him properly.

"Yeah, I'm fine. Leg's just a bit sore."

I noticed then that he was holding something. "What did you find?"

"Oh," he said, glancing toward the older lady he been speaking to. "Betty here thought I might like this."

He held out what she'd given him. It was a Christmas ornament. An angel, carved out of wood and painted gold.

It was bigger than his hand; the angel's wings were outstretched and she had a serene look on her face. It looked old, a little worn as though it was well loved, and it was beautiful.

"She said I could have it," Richard explained.

"That's not exactly true," Betty said from behind the counter. "I found that angel thrown in with all the other Christmas decorations, but no one knows where it came from. It wasn't in the bag with the others when we got it. It's like it just appeared overnight, and I said to Macy that I'd keep it aside for someone special. I thought this angel is just waiting for the right person to come along. Someone who needs an angel's help." She gave a determined nod toward Richard. "And then this nice young man tells me he's just returned from that horrible war. My Harold fought in the Second World War so I know well enough the angel found her someone special to look after this Christmas."

Richard's eyes were glassy. He was clearly touched by her words and her generosity. "Thank you," he said quietly.

She popped the angel in a bag for him. "Just remember," she said. "I'm gifting it to you. When you no longer need her help, you make sure you pass her along to someone who does."

Richard nodded solemnly. "I will."

She rang up our other items, which Kat and I paid for, then she wished us a Merry Christmas. "Same to you," I said in return.

We made our way out of the store onto the sidewalk. The wind had picked up and there was a chill in the air. The blue sky was gone, and in its place were dark and gloomy clouds with the threat of rain. We'd only done a few steps when I said, "Oh, I must've left my wallet. You two keep going and I'll catch up." I turned quickly and ran back into the store before Richard could question me. I found the box and the photo frames I'd stashed and took them to the counter.

"Did you forget something?" Betty asked.

"Yes. I wanted to grab these for my friend as a gift, but I didn't want him to see." She rung up the items, wrapped them in some tissue paper, and bagged them. "Thank you again for the angel. It was very kind of you, and it meant a lot to him."

"My pleasure, dear," she said sweetly. "I would guess that boy has been through hell, so he's going to need some good friends like you around him."

"Good friends and the lucky Christmas angel," I said.

She beamed up at me. "Merry Christmas."

I took my bags and left the store with a smile. Yes, Richard had been through hell, but he was home now. And I was now more determined to make this the best Christmas ever.

But I turned the corner, and what I saw made my stomach drop to my feet. Richard was huddled on the sidewalk with his back to the wall and his hands over his ears. Kat stood over him looking around, helpless and scared to death. I hadn't even noticed the noise overhead. But then I looked up and I saw it. A news channel helicopter flew overhead just above the buildings, so close I could see the pop rivets in the undercarriage.

And Richard was screaming.

CHAPTER TEN

RICHARD

I DON'T REMEMBER what happened.

I could remember leaving the store and being happy and excited for Christmas. The gift of the Christmas angel was an unexpected surprise, and I could remember feeling positive and looking forward to spending Christmas with Gary and Kat.

I could remember walking farther on with Kat when Gary had run back into the store to get his wallet, and we got around the corner and Kat was telling me where she was going to put the Christmas decorations.

And then everything went hazy. There was noise and fear. Like I somehow just transported back to Vietnam. The city of San Francisco disappeared around me, and I was back in a jungle, and there was a barking M16 and Jackson was on the radio yelling for an air raid, and there was the smell of blood and gunpowder. And screaming. So much screaming.

And then there was silence and the darkness, and when the haze cleared in my mind, I was back in the apartment, in Gary's bed.

My leg hurt like it was a fresh wound. I had a blinding headache. I felt nauseous. My heart felt too heavy for my chest. My lungs felt too small. Tears burned in my eyes, someone far away squeezed my hand, and when the darkness came, I went with it willingly.

WHEN I WOKE UP, the first thing I saw was the gold Christmas angel ornament. She now stood on the bedside table, her wings outstretched, watching over me.

"Hey," a soft voice said beside me. Gentle fingers found my hair, and when I looked at Gary, he smiled. "How you feeling?"

"Awful." My voice cracked. "My leg…"

Gary nodded. "You were crouching down, trying to make yourself smaller. I think you might have put some pressure on your injury, stretched it."

"I was?"

He nodded. "You don't remember?"

I shook my head and put my hands to my forehead. "My head aches."

"Want me to take a look at your leg? I can change the dressing for you."

"You don't have to do that."

"I don't have to. I want to. I want to look after you."

"I'm sorry," I offered weakly. "I don't know what happened back there."

"I do. That damned helicopter flew overhead and scared the shit out of you. It put you right back in the war."

I nodded and fought back tears as I began to remember. "I thought I was back there. It felt like it. I'm really sorry."

"Please don't apologize. You did nothing wrong."

"How did I get home?"

"I helped you. And Kat. We got you back here, no worries."

"Oh God." I covered my eyes with my hand.

"Hey," Gary said, gently prying my hand away. He threaded our fingers. "Don't be embarrassed."

That was easier said than done.

"How about I run your bath?. We can check your leg, and redress it when you get out. Kat is making a big pot of soup, so you can rest in bed and I'll spoon-feed it to you."

I almost smiled. "I can feed myself."

"I know you can. But I want to do it for you. I want to look after you because that's what you do when the person you love is having a shitty day."

"Is that what this is? A shitty day?"

Gary nodded. "Yep." He leaned down and kissed my forehead. "I'll go run you that bath."

I watched Gary walk out and noticed then the rain-splattered window, and suddenly a warm bath, a soft bed, and a bowl of soup sounded like heaven. I sat up in bed and pulled the covers back, then almost had to lift my left leg onto the floor. Pain bit into my leg like the shrapnel did and I could feel the color run from my face. I took some deep breaths but it did nothing to help. When Gary came back into the room, I didn't even have to ask him to get my pills. He took one look at me, threw the towel he was holding onto the bed, and grabbed me two pills and a glass of water.

"Here, baby," he whispered. "Take these."

I swallowed them down greedily. "Thank you."

He helped me undress, pulling my shirt over my head, then helped me to my feet and carefully undid my trousers, then ever so gently pulled them down my thighs. I half expected to see red blotches in the bandages around my thigh, but there were none. Gary carefully unwrapped the bandages and slowly revealed my thigh.

I hated the look of it, even on a good day. But now it was red and hot to the touch. It was angry where I had stretched the skin. There was no way I would have normally crouched down on my haunches. My leg wouldn't have let me.

But when that helicopter went over…

I guess it was proof the human mind could do crazy things. I had no recollection of my leg even hurting when I was on the street. My mind was too busy thinking it had gone back to Vietnam to feel physical pain, but I sure felt it now.

Gary had never seen my injury up this close. I'd always had the bandages on or was wrapping it when he came into the room. But as he knelt before me now and inspected the lumps and indentations, the ugly scarring, there was no shock or horror on his face. Only concern. "There are no tears or ruptures," he said looking it over. "But after your bath, we can wrap it up tight again. And I want you to have complete bed rest for a few days at least."

"Yes, doctor," I said as a joke.

He stood to his full height and kissed me with smiling lips. "Need help getting out of those briefs?"

"Yes," I didn't hesitate to answer.

He slid his fingers under the elastic and slid my briefs down, being extra careful of my thigh. I expected him to touch my dick or maybe even nudge it with his nose, but he didn't. He simply stood, wrapped a towel around my waist, and led me to the bathroom. "I'm a little disappointed," I said once the door was closed behind us. "I was naked in front of you and you didn't touch me."

Gary smirked and shut off the water. He checked the

temperature of the bath, then removed my towel so I was naked again. "And I won't until I know you're not in any pain."

"Those pills are already kicking in," I said.

"You know what I mean."

And I did. He was right. I wasn't up for anything sexual, not physically, not mentally, not emotionally. I sat in the bath while Gary sat on the edge of the tub and washed me down with a cloth. Then he helped me out of the bath, got me all dried off, and helped me put on clean underwear and a T-shirt. He rewrapped my leg; then helped me back into bed.

I sat propped up against the headboard and let him spoon-feed me some soup. He might have said he wanted to look after me, but I also needed him to do it. Sure, I was physically capable of feeding myself, but I didn't realize how much I needed to feel loved and cared for.

When I couldn't eat any more, he put the bowl on the side table and climbed into bed with me. He pulled me into his arms so my head was on his chest. He ran his fingers through my hair and traced patterns on my back. The pills had taken effect, the pain was gone, and I was feeling a little spaced out.

"Thank you," I murmured. "For everything."

He squeezed me. "You're very welcome."

"I'd be so lost without you." I could feel the chemical sleep dragging me under. The last thing I saw was the gold Christmas angel on the bedside table watching over me. "Now I have two angels."

I SLEPT right through till morning. The pills had worn off,

the pain in my leg was back with a vengeance, and I needed to pee.

Gary was still asleep, but he stirred when I got out of bed. "What's wrong?" he croaked.

"Nothing. Just need the bathroom." My cane was at the end of the bed, so I grabbed it and went across the hall. I still felt like I'd been hit by a truck; I think it was a kind of mental fatigue or something I recalled doctors talking about, because it was a tiredness I could feel in my bones. After I'd peed and brushed my teeth, I climbed back into bed. Gary slid his arm around me, pulled my back to his front—the strength and scent of all man surrounded me—and I dozed off again.

He might have been joking about bed rest for a few days, but the way I felt, I certainly wasn't going to argue. I ended up staying in bed most of the day, dozing and lethargic, and Gary came in every so often to check on me, feed me, kiss me. But by mid-afternoon, I was sick of the bedroom walls and I went in search of company.

I used the bathroom, then limped out to the living room with my cane. I noticed the Christmas tree we chose was sitting in the corner, still undecorated. I guessed my little episode in the street yesterday had thrown a wrench in the works. "Oh, hey," Gary said, coming out of the kitchen. "What are you doing up?"

"I'm sick of being in bed."

"Would the sofa be more comfortable?" he asked. "I can grab you a pillow and blanket and you can watch TV."

"Or I could just sit with you."

He gave me a hug. "Or that."

"Where's Kat?" I hadn't seen her since my episode with the helicopter.

"She went out for lunch with some friends. It usually means she'll be gone for hours, but she'll be back soon."

He looked back to the kitchen. "I was going to make burgers for dinner. How does that sound?"

"Perfect. Need me to help?"

"I'm almost done, but I'm sure I can find something… like maybe wash a few dishes." He winked and gave me a kiss. "Oh, and I'll make some popcorn after because *Cactus Flower* is the Sunday night movie."

I had no idea what *Cactus Flower* was. I was so out of the loop on movies, television, and music. But it didn't matter what it was. As long as I was with him. "Sounds perfect."

Gary finished making the hamburger mix and I did the dishes, and when we were done, he wrapped his arms around me right there in the kitchen. We stood there in that embrace for so long, and I was warm and felt so safe, I almost fell asleep against him.

"Come on," he said with a laugh. "To the couch with you." I went willingly, and by the time I'd pulled my bad leg up and got comfortable, Gary came back out with a pillow and a blanket. "Hey, make room for me."

I shuffled forward a bit and he jumped up behind me, slid one of his legs on either side of me, and I was suddenly resting my back against his chest. I relaxed against him immediately and the weight of his arms felt wonderful around me.

"I don't know why I'm so exhausted," I said.

"You went through quite an ordeal yesterday," he murmured with a kiss to the back of my head.

"They said it could happen," I admitted quietly. "The doctors, in the hospital. That certain things could affect me like that. Loud, sudden noises, helicopters, fireworks. They called it something, but I can't remember…"

"Having a shitty day."

I chuckled. "Um, not sure that was it."

"But that's what we can call it. And if you have more shitty days, we'll deal with them. Just know that if you have one, or a hundred, it's okay. It's not your fault."

"How do you know to say exactly what I need to hear?"

He sighed and nuzzled into my hair. "Because I love you."

I closed my eyes. "Remember when I was in the hospital, you once told me when I got out and moved in with you, we would have privacy to do whatever we want. That we could just be us."

"I remember."

"It seemed so unlikely. So far-fetched that two men could live together. Be together. Free to kiss, make love—"

"Cuddle on the sofa," he added.

"Yes. Being here with you, just like this. I never dreamed it would come true."

"Mmm," he hummed against my head. And for a long while, neither of us spoke. We just lay there, finding peace in each other's company. "How's your leg?" he asked eventually.

"Sore."

"Want me to get your pills?"

"Nah. I'll take them when we go to bed."

A key rattled in the door, and Kat said, "It's just me," as she came inside.

"Hey," Gary said.

"Hi," I added.

She dumped her handbag on the other sofa and came over to us. She looked directly at me. "How are you feeling?"

"Better, thank you. Still tired though, and I might have set my leg back three months in healing, but I'm better." I tried to smile for her. "Thank you for being there, and I'm sorry for putting you through that. It can't have been pretty."

She rubbed my arm. "It was no problem. A bit scary, I'll admit, but I was glad I was there so we could get you home." Then she turned around and scanned the living room. "We need to decorate the tree! It's Christmas in a week! I want this apartment to look like the North Pole!"

"Oh," I said. "Gary had plans to make burgers and watch a movie."

Kat grinned. "Excellent. Decorations, burgers, movie. That's our night."

She wasted no time in pulling out the bags of decorations and Gary got up to help her. "Come on," he said to me. "You're helping too."

"I'm a bit of a cripple," I said, slowly getting to my feet.

"You are not," Gary said, holding out some tinsel to me. "You're very capable of doing anything you put your mind to. And I've told you before not to call the guy I love that word."

I took the tinsel and fought a smile. I loved how he treated me as though I was normal. As though I wasn't injured, and like I was the same man I was before. Using my cane, I stepped in closer to him and kissed his cheek and the three of us set about making the apartment as Christmassy as we could.

We stood the tree in the corner next to the television, added tinsel and ornaments and lights. Kat set up some reindeer figurines in a sleigh formation on the windowsill and Gary tacked the three stockings underneath it. Kat added some Christmas lights, and there were Santa candles and the small plastic tree for the table and garlands over the doorways. For a few dollars at the thrift shop, it looked pretty darn good.

We ate our burgers, which were delicious, and we settled on the sofas to watch the movie. Gary made popcorn, and although my leg hurt and I had to fight nodding off, I really did have a lovely night.

The fact that this was my life now was something I'd always be amazed at. Despite my physical and psychological injuries, I was living my life as a gay man—living as my true self—and that was something I'd never take for granted.

I must've dozed off for the end of the movie because I woke up to Gary's gentle touch and his whispered words. "Come on, baby. Let's get you to bed."

We used the bathroom and brushed our teeth, and I all but fell onto the edge of the bed as I sat down. "I'm so fucking tired," I mumbled. "I don't think I was this tired in the hospital."

Gary closed the door and came over to stand between my legs; then he pulled my head against his belly and stroked my hair. "Give yourself time to heal. There's no time limit on it. However long it takes. And anyway, I have to work the next four days so you'll have plenty of time to sleep and rest, okay?"

I nodded. "You're a very patient man."

He rubbed my back. "I am. Especially if it's worth waiting for," he said with a laugh. "And you totally are."

I looked up at him, my chin resting on his stomach. "You're kind of great, you know that?"

"I do, but you can keep telling me. I won't mind," he said with a grin. Then he noticed the angel still sitting on the bedside table. Gary leaned over and picked it up. "Oh, we forgot about this. It should go on the tree."

"Can she stay beside our bed?" I asked. "We can put her on the tree on Christmas Eve, if that's okay. My mom would have an angel on the mantelpiece until Christmas

Eve dinner; then she'd put it on the tree. Apparently her mother and grandmother did that. It's probably silly…"

He smiled warmly at me. "That's not silly. It's perfect. And anyway, I like the idea of this angel watching over you while you rest." He put the angel back on the table, and I leaned across and turned her around so she wasn't privy to what I wanted to do to Gary. I ran my hands down over his ass and the back of his thighs. I was at a very convenient height, and when I eyed his crotch, then met his gaze, he caught on. "You were falling asleep a few minutes ago. Is your leg sore?"

I licked my lips and began to undo his fly. "A little," I lied. It was aching but I had more immediate needs. "I really want this. Then I can take my pills and we'll both sleep better."

I opened his fly roughly and shoved his briefs down to free his dick. He liked being manhandled; his groan and the jerk of his cock told me he liked it a lot. I wasted no time sucking him into my mouth. He grew hard fast, and although he was gentle with his hands, he thrust into my mouth, over and over, until he was rock-hard and his thrusts became a little harder and faster. "Richard, baby. I'm gonna come."

I sucked him in as far as I could take him, looked up at his face to find him watching me. "Oh God," he murmured. "That's so hot."

I groaned around him and he let his head fall back as he came down my throat. He shuddered and moaned, and when I pulled off, he took hold of my face and kissed me. He must've been able to taste himself because he hummed, then he ended the kiss with a smile. "Your turn?"

I shook my head. "No, that was just for you."

He kissed me again and stroked his thumb across my cheek. "Get into bed," he murmured, tucking himself back into his jeans. "I'll get your pills for you." He went to leave the room but stopped. He turned the angel back around so she faced me, and I laughed. I lifted my leg onto the mattress and settled into bed, and took my pills when he brought me a glass of water. He climbed in behind me, wrapped me up in his arms so I was in the only safe place I'd ever known, and we both slept like logs.

I SPENT ALL the next day on the couch, watching TV, dozing, resting, healing, but the day after that I was getting restless. I felt much better, and while my leg had appreciated the recovery, I needed to stretch it.

I also needed to get Gary and Kat a Christmas gift each. And, if my leg was up for it, I'd stop in at the market and grab something to cook for dinner. I didn't have a lot of money, but I wanted to show them how much I appreciated them.

It was Christmas after all. And this was the first year since I was a kid that Christmas incited any kind of hope.

Gone was the judgment, the scorn. Gone was the church that told me I was sick, mentally disturbed, an abomination, and gone was the dread they might have been right.

No, this Christmas there was love and hope and acceptance of who I really was.

I sat on the bed to pull on my boots and smiled back at the Christmas angel who watched over me. "This is the first Christmas of the rest of my life," I told her. "I need to make it special. I need to show Gary how much I love him."

And just then, a beam of sunlight shined through the window and caught the angel in its glow. She looked ethereal, even a little bit magic. And I knew it was just the light and the shadows on her face, but she really appeared to smile, as though she somehow knew.

I stood up and put on my coat, and with a newfound determination, I left the apartment and went out.

CHAPTER ELEVEN

GARY

COMING HOME from work had never been so high up on my agenda. When I was in college, going back to my dorm room had been the last thing on my mind. I wanted to hang out with friends, meet in coffee houses or diners, discussing current affairs and how technology was going to change the world.

Now all I wanted to do was go home, throw my arms around Richard, and spend the night cuddling up on the couch.

Don't get me wrong. I loved my job. Technology *was* going to change the world, and being part of a group of like-minded, driven people in what could be the beginning of a very big thing was invigorating. But being greeted by Richard with a kiss and hug was by far the highlight of my day.

He'd spent all day yesterday taking it easy, but he was determined to go out today. He said he was ready and I had to trust his judgment. I made sure he had my work phone number and told him to call if he needed, but I didn't hear from him. So I was anxious to get home, and the bus ride home seemed to stretch on forever. I had horror scenarios playing in my mind that he'd had another incident, another shitty day, as I'd called it. Maybe another helicopter went overhead, or maybe a car backfired, or maybe some random stranger decided they didn't like to see a man with a cane and harassed him… Okay, so that was unlikely, but I couldn't help but worry.

I hurried down the block and raced up the stairs to our door, fumbled with the key, and finally pushed my way inside. "Richard?" I tried to sound calm.

He limped out of the kitchen with his cane and smiled when he saw me. "Oh hey, you're a little early."

I peeled off my coat and tossed it on the sofa, then went to him and cupped his face and gave him a soft kiss. "I ran."

"What for?"

"I missed you," I answered, only a half lie.

His smile widened. "You were worried."

"I was. I didn't hear from you, and I knew you were going out."

His smile became a frown. "You told me to call if something was wrong. I didn't mean to make you worry."

"Oh, it's not your fault. I have an overactive imagination." I tilted his face up some more and kissed him again, a little deeper this time. "I missed you though. That part was true."

He slow blinked, his cheeks a little flushed. "I missed you too."

I slid my hands down his back and pulled our hips together. "You look tired."

"I am a bit tired," he admitted. "I walked a ways. Well, for me." Then he licked his lips and smiled. "Um, I don't think you were done kissing me."

I chuckled. "Is that right?"

He nodded and I captured his mouth with mine again, this time taking my time and kissing him thoroughly. We were both breathless when we pulled apart, but I suddenly noticed something I hadn't before. "What can I smell?"

"Oh," he said, turning toward the kitchen. "I made dinner. It's supposed to be chicken supreme, but I don't know…"

"It smells amazing," I said. I opened the oven door and inhaled. "Looks good too. You made this?"

He gave an uncertain one-shoulder shrug. "Well, yeah. The lady at the grocery store told me what to do. I must've looked lost in the meat department. They had a sale on chicken, so I was looking… Anyway, she came up to me and asked if I needed help." Then he laughed. "Boy, isn't that a loaded question. I don't know the first thing about cooking. So she told me a fail-safe recipe or two."

"She did?"

He nodded with a laugh. "Tomorrow night I'm going to try to replicate her grandmother's Creole pork and potatoes."

I laughed as well and pulled him in for another hug. "I'm so glad you had a good day."

He sighed against me. "I did. No mishaps, but I'm tired. I spent half a year in Vietnam walking miles every day with a pack that weighed almost more than me. Now I can't even walk the block without it knocking me around."

I pulled back so I could look him in the eyes. "And you spent months bedridden in the hospital. Don't be so hard on yourself. I can see you improving every day."

"You can?"

I nodded and pecked his lips again. "Definitely."

This seemed to please him, but then his cheeks flushed deep pink. "Improved enough that you might want to have your way with me?"

My eyes went wide. "Now?"

"No, not right now. Kat will be home soon, but maybe later." He swallowed hard, clearly embarrassed. "I mean, what we've been doing is great but… I just thought…"

"You just thought what?"

"You haven't wanted to have me… that way. The way you did at Woodstock. And I wondered if it was because…"

Oh, okay. I hadn't expected that. "Well," I started, trying to word this right. "Don't ever think I don't want you, because I do." I took his hand and put it to my crotch so he could feel what just being close to him did to me. "You turn me on like crazy. I didn't want to push you for sex because I don't want to rush you or hurt your leg. What if I grip you too hard or what if I lose myself in the moment and push your leg too high or too hard."

He frowned. "I hadn't thought of that. Well, I mean I had. Kind of. I just thought there would be ways I could lie down so it doesn't hurt."

I couldn't help but smirk. "You've been thinking about it, have you?"

He nodded and tried to look away, but I held his face. "Been thinking about it a lot, actually."

I slowly walked him backward until his ass hit the kitchen cabinets near the sink, and when he could go no farther, I pressed my body against his. "That's so hot," I murmured and crushed my mouth to his. He groaned as our tongues touched, but before things could get too heated, we heard Kat's key at the door.

She came inside, dumped her coat, and sighed. "I'm beat, and I need to take these shoes off. They're killing me," she said, then disappeared into her room. Thankfully she hadn't seemed to notice through the kitchen door, us pressed up against the cupboard.

I chuckled and took a small step back. I readjusted myself and tried to will my body back under control. Richard licked his lips and smiled just as Kat walked back out. "Please tell me whatever smells so good is our dinner tonight?"

Richard grinned. "It sure is. Oh, that reminds me," he said, looking at us both. "I wanted to ask what we wanted to have for Christmas dinner. I can grab it tomorrow or on Christmas Eve. I thought if we each suggested something, it'd be nice."

"Oh," Kat said. "Didn't I tell you? I'll be spending Christmas Day with my Great Aunt Rose. She lives in San Jose, and I promised my mom I would."

"Oh," Richard said, clearly disappointed. She'd told me, but I must've forgotten to pass the news on.

Kat noticed Richard's deflated smile. "What if we make our dinner on Christmas Eve and even have a fancy breakfast on Christmas Day. I'll have to leave mid-morning, and that will give you two the day alone together." She waggled her eyebrows. "How does that sound?"

"Sounds good," I replied. "Christmas breakfast isn't too conventional, but then again, neither are we."

Richard smiled genuinely now. "Perfect."

By the time we'd eaten and cleaned up after dinner, we'd only been on the sofa for about half an hour before Richard's blinks were getting longer. But every time he'd move, he'd wince at his leg. "Come on," I said, getting to my feet, then pulling him to his. "Pain pills and bedtime for you."

"What time is it?" he asked. He sat on the edge of the bed and I handed him two of his pills and a glass of water.

"Almost eight."

"Ugh, it's so early."

I kissed his forehead. "Go to sleep, baby. You're so tired

you can't keep your eyes open." Then I whispered, "There'll be no sex tonight, but who knows. Maybe Santa will come early."

He snorted and lay down. "He won't be the only one."

I barked out a laugh and turned the Christmas angel so she faced him more directly. "Be careful who hears you. This Christmas angel might tell Santa you've been a naughty boy."

He was smiling, though his eyes were half-closed. "Too late. I've already told her what I want."

"Are you going to tell me what you want Santa to bring?" I asked.

"I already have," he mumbled.

Chuckling, I leaned down and kissed his temple. "You want sex for Christmas?" But his only reply was a quiet snore.

WORK WAS BUSY, finalizing invoices and orders before most businesses shut down over Christmas and New Year's. We'd had a small staff Christmas party in our break room during our lunch hour. There were Santa hats and tinsel and reindeer antlers and red noses, and I left the office with a small Christmas bonus, feeling happy, festive, and really eager to get home.

I had four days off and intended to spend every minute with Richard. He hadn't mentioned his sex request again from the night before last. He'd been tired by the time we went to bed last night as well. I'd propped him up in bed and worshipped his body, bringing us both to climax with my hand. It seemed all he had energy for, but I was hoping he'd rested well. It was the night before Christmas Eve, and I knew Richard was trying to make our Christmas Eve dinner something special for all of us, and I wanted that too.

I smiled as I climbed the stairs to our apartment, and I heard his voice as I unlocked the door. He was talking on the phone, with wide eyes and a weird smile. "Oh, he's home!" he said to whomever he was talking to. "Let me put him on for you. … Yes, ma'am. The pleasure was all mine. … Yes, I'll be sure to mention it. Thank you, and a Merry Christmas to you too." By this time, he was red with embarrassment, and he handed the phone receiver out to me. "It's your mom."

I laughed and took the phone. "Mom, have you been giving Richard the third degree?"

She laughed. "Oh, Gary, he sounds like the sweetest boy. And his manners!"

I slid my free hand around Richard's neck and gently pulled him into my chest so he could bury his face in my sweater and die of embarrassment. "He is, Mom. The sweetest boy."

"When do we get to meet him? It's about time we met this young man."

"Soon. You get to meet him real soon, I promise."

Richard pulled away and gawped at me, making me laugh. "I'm glad you called tonight," I said to her. "I need your recipe for your apple pie. We're gonna make our first Christmas dinner together something special, and there isn't anything as special as your apple pie."

Richard gave me a smile, with cheeks flushed pink and his eyes warm with love. "Really?" he whispered, and I nodded.

"Oh honey, that's so sweet!" Mom replied. "You'll need a pen. Have you got a pen?"

After I hung the receiver in the cradle, Richard

grabbed my beard in his hands and brought me in for a kiss. "We're gonna make an apple pie?"

I grinned at him. "Yep. I got a little Christmas bonus today. It's not enough to buy anything fancy, but you're trying to plan a special dinner and I thought a hot apple pie and ice cream, and maybe some cider, would make it perfect."

"It sounds perfect!" he replied. "And your mom! Oh my gosh, Gary, she was talking to me like me being your boyfriend was the most natural thing in the world! She was asking me all about my leg and how I was finding San Francisco and how you were treating me." He shook his head. "I'm still stunned."

His smile also told me he was very happy. "Of course she did! She wants to meet you."

"That's what she said. She told me I had to tell you that she wants to meet me."

"And my dad. Both of them," I added.

Richard froze, then blanched. "Your… dad? He knows? I mean you said he does, but he wants to meet me?"

I kissed him and gave him a long, strong hug. "Of course he does."

"And he's okay with it? He knows we're…"

I nodded into his neck. "Yes, baby. He knows." I kissed the skin below his ear. "He wasn't too fond of the idea in the beginning, of me liking boys, but he realized I'm still the same as I was before I'd told him. Plus my mom told me later that when they were in college, they had a certain *ménage à trois* with a football quarterback, and he'd enjoyed every minute."

Richard stared at me. Then he blinked, and his mouth opened but it seemed words failed him. Then he shook his head as if to kickstart his brain. "She told you that? About what they've done in the bedroom?"

"Apparently this wasn't in a bedroom. It was in a pool-room," I added with a laugh. "And yes, she told me. And she reminded my dad of the fact and he didn't have a problem with me liking boys after that."

Richard stared again, then roared with laughter. "I cannot believe you've discussed anything *like* that with your parents!"

"I take it you didn't?"

"Never! My parents would've called a priest for an exorcism if I mentioned sex. I'm sure my mother would have me believe I was conceived through the Holy Spirit. Like Jesus. Because sex was forbidden."

I let my head fall back and groaned. "God, your parents must be miserable."

"Well, they weren't having threesomes in college, that's for sure," he said with a grin. "They never went to college. They met at church."

I slung my arms around his shoulders and pressed my lips to his. "Anyway, yes, my folks want to meet you. Is that okay with you?"

"I've never met anyone's parents before," he whispered. "Let alone the parents of a man. Who know we're together, and we share a bed." He cringed. "Would they really be okay with it?"

I nodded.

He seemed suddenly nervous. He let out a breath and licked his lips. "It's a big step and I've always thought that meeting parents was something people did when they were serious, and you know, getting married."

"Well, we can't get married. Not yet. But if we could, I'd do it in a heartbeat. That's how serious I am about you. About us."

"Not yet?"

"One day I bet we will," I answered. "The world is changing. It might not be anytime soon, but one day we'll be treated the same as other couples."

"You really believe that?"

"I have to. I have to believe that."

He broke out a killer-watt smile. "Then I would love to meet your parents. I'll be scared and nervous as hell, but I'll do it."

"Good! It probably won't be until Easter or even my birthday next year. We have plenty of time."

"Your birthday's July, right?"

I nodded. "Yep. July twenty-fourth," I reminded him. Then I held up the recipe I'd written out. "We need to brave the stores in the morning so we can get the ingredients for this. I thought we could make it together. Make it our thing to do every year, like a tradition."

His eyes welled with tears and he nodded. "Sounds perfect."

"Oh, baby, don't cry," I said, pulling him against me again. I knew talking about family and Christmas had to hurt when his family had basically washed their hands of him. "I didn't mean to upset you."

"Happy tears," he sniffed.

I pulled back and put my hand to his face so I could see his eyes. "You sure?"

He nodded, teary, but smiling. "The happiest. I love you, Gary Fairchild."

"I love you too, Richard Ronsman." I kissed him again, but then the oven timer buzzed and told us that some lady from the grocery store's grandmother's ground beef casserole recipe was done.

SHOPPING ON CHRISTMAS Eve was crazy. We got there just after opening and there were already people fighting over turkeys, and I thought they might trigger a negative reaction in Richard, but he was more amused than scared.

"I've never seen two women want to duke it out over frozen birds before," he said, watching them as we walked past. The store manager was trying to wrangle them as I ushered Richard into the first aisle. We soon filled our basket with our list of ingredients, and we found some discounted decorations and Santa hats, and I grabbed two bottles of apple cider, and we made the trek home.

"Oh," I said as we passed a drugstore. "I need to grab something real quick." I offloaded my bag into Richard's arm, which he almost dropped as he struggled with his cane and his own grocery bag. I grinned over my shoulder at him as I went inside. I bought a small bottle of perfume for Kat, along with some lubricant, which was packaged into a brown paper bag by the young clerk, and I went back out to Richard.

"I almost dropped the wine," he said. "Warn a cripple next time, will you, before you throw things at him."

I chuckled and took the bag from him. "You're not a cripple. And I've told you before"—I leaned in real close —"not to call the man I love that word."

He tried to be mad but he fought a smile. "I didn't know you needed medication," he said as we began to walk home.

"Medication?"

"Yeah, from the drugstore."

I laughed. "I didn't buy medication. I bought some lubricant."

Richard almost stumbled, and he shot me a glare. "Jesus."

"You brought it up," I said with a laugh.

"Warn a man next time before you say stuff like that."

I grinned the whole way home.

And I grinned the whole time we made homemade apple pie, and we laughed as we prepared everything for dinner and put the turkey in the oven to cook. We rested after lunch; Richard needed to put his foot up so the three of us watched Christmas movies all afternoon. The weather had turned cold, wind howled against the window, but it really set the scene for Christmas Eve. We had pillows and blankets, Kat made eggnog, and we ate bowls of popcorn. Richard lay with his head on my chest with my arms around him, and I really could not have picked a better way to spend Christmas Eve.

"I know it's Christmas and not Thanksgiving," Richard said. "But I'm really thankful I'm in San Francisco and not Connecticut. If we still lived back east we'd be under four feet of snow."

That made me laugh. "Ain't that the truth."

Kat agreed. "I don't miss shoveling sidewalks and driveways, that's for sure."

"My dad would have me shoveling snow for hours. My feet and hands would be frozen solid," Richard said.

"That's terrible," Kat said. "And mean."

Richard snorted. "Then I'd have to go do the pastor's driveway too."

"You didn't have a plow for that?" I asked.

"Yeah. Dad did. But making me do it the way he had to do it when he was a boy would teach me to appreciate it later."

Kat gasped. "Now that's just being horrible."

"I didn't mind. The pastor was a jerk but his neighbor was cute. He'd watch me shovel for hours."

I laughed and kissed the side of his head. "If only your dad knew."

Richard smiled but we fell silent after that. "I should probably call them," he said. "You know, for Christmas and all."

"Anything you want," I murmured. "If you want to call them or if you don't, it's completely up to you."

He sighed. "I just need to decide which day I want to ruin. I've had such a perfect day today, but I doubt I'll want to ruin Christmas Day either."

Kat gave him a sympathetic smile. "Why don't you call them after you've had a glass of cider or two with dinner. Might make it a little easier."

"Good idea," he replied, his good mood deflated. I tightened my hold on him and kissed the top of his head.

Kat stood up and clapped her hands together, trying to be cheery. "How about we have this amazing dinner you two spent all day cooking. We'll have more eggnog and drink some apple cider. We can put the Christmas tree lights on, and if we get drunk enough, we can sing carols."

Richard laughed and got to his feet. He shuffled around on his good leg and held his hand out. "Come on," he said with a smile that gave me butterflies. "It's Christmastime."

So with another Christmas movie on the television, we turned the Christmas tree lights on, sat down at our Christmas-decorated table to one of the best Christmas dinners and apple pies I'd ever had.

We ate, we drank, we laughed. And yes, when the second bottle of cider was almost empty, we sang Christmas carols—very badly, I might add. But we laughed and laughed, and there was so much love in that room I was sure Neil Armstrong could have seen it from space.

I danced with Kat while Richard sat and watched—and laughed until he cried—and when I pulled him to his feet to dance with him, he objected at first. But then Kat changed the music to a slower song, and as Bing Crosby crooned out from the record player, I slow danced with Richard in our living room.

I didn't know what Kat was doing when she pulled a dining chair over to us, but she stood up tall and held out a piece of the garland over our heads. I glanced up at it and laughed. "I think that's supposed to be mistletoe," I whispered in Richard's ear. "Ever been kissed under mistletoe?"

He shook his head and we stopped dancing. I lifted his chin and kissed him with all the love I had. I must've kissed him so good he forgot where he was because he groaned and started to pull my shirt up.

"Okay guys, I don't need the full show," Kat said with a laugh, jumping down off the chair.

Richard pulled away, stunned and a little horrified at his behavior. "I'm sorry, I…"

Kat laughed. "Don't ever be sorry. I'll take love over hate any day."

I pulled him into me once more and we swayed a little. "I should call my folks."

I kissed him. "We'll start cleaning up the kitchen, give you some privacy."

He nodded and I spun Kat into the kitchen, making her laugh. We washed and dried and tidied up the kitchen while he spoke quietly on the phone to his parents. We tried not to listen, but it was a bit hard not to hear.

"I'm still in San Francisco," he said. "No, I'm staying here." There was a long pause. "Hard on you? What about hard on me? I almost died in Vietnam and then again in the hospital. I can't work the farm because I can hardly walk. Not that you'd know. You never came to visit. You called once. That's not what love is. That's not unconditional. It's never been unconditional." Another long pause. "I can't do that. … I'm sorry you feel that way."

Kat reached out and squeezed my hand. "Go to him," she whispered. "I'll finish up in here."

I gave her a thankful nod, put the dish towel on the counter, and went into the living room. He was sitting on the arm of the sofa, the spiral phone cord stretched straight. He had his head down and I couldn't see his face.

"Well, I just thought you might like to know that I'm okay," Richard said quietly into the phone. There was another pause and I put my hand in his hair. He looked up at me and gave me a sad smile. I traced my thumb along his cheek.

"I love you," I mouthed to him.

He smiled, though it was marked by sadness. "I, uh, look, I have to go. Tell Dad I said Merry Christmas. If it means anything." He shook his head. "You know what, Mom. I need to tell you something. I'm happy. For the first time in my life, I'm truly happy. I don't expect you to understand, but as a parent—if all any parent wants is for their child to be happy—then know that I am."

He smiled, properly this time, and held the phone receiver out. "She hung up."

"Oh baby." I put my hand to his face. "I'm sorry."

"I'm not," he said with a sigh. "I needed to say that. I've needed to say that for a long time. I mean, it's not the happy ending I wanted. Well, not with them anyway. But I can't change their minds, and I won't live a lie anymore."

"I'm proud of you," I whispered.

He stood slowly and put his head to my chest. "I'm sorry I couldn't be the son they wanted, but I can't be someone I'm not."

I slid my arms around him and held him tight. "You don't have to be anyone but you."

He lifted his head and met my gaze. "You've never wanted me to be anything I'm not."

"Because you're perfect just the way you are." I kissed him softly. "Can I get you anything? More cider or more eggnog?"

"Eggnog sounds good."

When I came back out of the kitchen with two glasses of eggnog, Richard was walking out of the hall, cane in one hand, the golden Christmas angel in the other. "We forgot about this," he said.

Kat followed me out. "Forgot about what?"

"Our Christmas angel," he answered. "We need to put it on the tree and make a wish."

"Who's going first?" I asked.

Richard hung his cane over a dining chair so he could take his eggnog and held out the angel to Kat. Then he put his arm around my waist. "Ladies first."

She took the ornament with a smile. "What do I do?"

"Hold it and make a wish," he said. "Then when we've all had a turn, we put her on top of the tree. Well, at least that's what my grandmother used to do."

Kat gave him a warm smile; then she closed her eyes for a second, and when she opened her eyes, she handed the ornament to me. "Your turn."

I looked at the angel, at her beautiful face, her wings… I closed my eyes, took a deep breath, and made my wish.

Then I handed it to Richard. He smiled at it, closed his eyes for a heartbeat, then looked at me and Kat. "Now we put her on the top of the tree." Once he had the angel situated, he slid his arm around my waist again and sipped his eggnog.

"Merry Christmas."

I held up my glass. "Merry Christmas."

Kat looked around and found the almost empty cider bottle on the table. She grabbed it and raised it, clinking our glasses. "Merry Christmas."

We all drank to that.

"What did you wish for, Kat?" I asked.

"Peace," she said simply. We drank to that too.

Then Richard leaned in real close and pressed his forehead to my jaw. His eyes were closed, his body pressed against mine. "So, what did you wish for?" he asked.

"I can't tell you that, or it won't come true." I ran my hand down his back and over his ass. "If it hasn't already."

He leaned into me and hummed.

Kat cleared her throat. "On that note, I will leave you two gentlemen to finish what you started. Goodnight! And don't be too naughty," she said with a wink. "Santa's watching!"

"Goodnight, Kat," I said.

"Goodnight," Richard said, but he didn't move from where he'd planted himself against me. She blew us a kiss and disappeared into her room.

I took Richard's eggnog and put our glasses on the table, then slid my hands down his sides and over his ass again. He loved it.

"What did you wish for?" I whispered.

"I didn't wish for anything." He looked up at me, his eyes full of desire. "I have everything I need. So I thanked the angel instead."

"You have everything you'll ever need?"

"Well, I have you. And you have lube." His cheeks flushed pink, but he held my gaze. "I need you to have me. The way you did at Woodstock."

I kissed him, slow and deep, until he moaned. I was breathless when we broke apart. "Then we should take it to our room. Unless you want to get on Santa's naughty list."

He laughed. "Oh boy, do I ever."

I handed him his cane and flipped off the lights,

leaving the living room aglow in Christmas tree lights. I took my time undressing him between gentle touches and deep kisses.

It had been so long since we'd done this, and that was the last time I'd done it, so I tried to keep myself in check. When I unbuttoned his shirt and kissed down his neck to his shoulder, he made this desperate whining sound that damn near brought me undone.

"I'm trying to go slow," I said breathily. "Or I won't even make it inside you."

He groaned, and his fingers dug into my sides. "Don't hold back," he whispered. "Don't go slow."

I licked a trail up to behind his ear. "Get on the bed."

He quickly complied, sitting first and then scooting back. "How do you want me?"

I shed my clothing as quickly as I could, so I was completely naked in front of him. "Just like that."

I grabbed the lube and threw it on the bedside, and I crawled up his legs, planting kisses as I went. His thigh was still bandaged, but I kissed up his inner thigh anyway. I nudged his cock with my nose, then licked his length, teasing him, before I made my way up his body to his mouth.

I kissed him, deep and slow, until he rolled his hips searching for touch. "Please, Gary. I need this."

I moved off him. "Roll onto your side," I urged him. He did as I asked, rolling onto his side so there was no pressure on his bandaged leg. "Is that okay?"

He arched his back, offering me his ass. "Yeah."

I fisted my cock first, giving the base a squeeze to stem the urgency. Then poured lube on my fingers and rubbed it over his hole, making him whimper. "You keep making noises like that, and you'll make me come," I whispered in his ear, then slipped a finger inside him.

He gasped and arched some more. He was so desperate, so deprived of what he really needed. "You want my cock instead?"

"Yes," he answered quickly. "Please Gary. I need it."

I slicked my cock with lube and added more to his hole, then pressed against him. "Like that?"

"Stop teasing me," he snapped, his patience gone.

So I pushed inside, just the head, breaching his tight ass so his breath caught and stuttered. I put a hand on his hip, careful of his injuries, and slowly pushed inside him. "You okay?"

He reached out and fisted the blankets, moaning long and low. "God yes." He took in some rapid breaths, and I wondered if it was too much for him. But then he breathed out slowly and he relaxed, and I slid farther in. "Feels so good," he mumbled.

I pulled out a little and pushed back in, deeper, and he moaned again. My chest was pressed to his back, and I kissed his shoulder, his neck. Then he started to jack himself. "Fuck, Richard, you're so hot. You make me wanna come, but I need you to come first."

He reacted to my words, writhing and meeting my thrusts. "Oh, Gary," he breathed my name. "More."

So I thrust a little harder, deeper, and sucked down on his neck, making him cry out. He went rigid and a strangled cry ripped from deep his chest as he came. He jerked on my cock, milking my orgasm out of me. I pushed in hard, one more time, and spilled inside him.

I tightened my arms around him, still trying to get closer. I kissed all the skin I could reach, and when our breathing had returned to normal, neither one of us moved. The alarm clock said 12:08. "Merry Christmas, baby."

He hummed sleepily. "Merry Christmas."

I peeled myself away, and when I looked back at him, I was struck at how beautiful he was. Naked, sleepy, smiling. I sat beside him. "Want me to get your pills?"

He shook his head. "No. I want you back in bed with your arms around me. 'S all I need."

I snuggled back in and pulled the blankets up, and he worked his way against me, as close as he could get. I kissed his forehead with smiling lips. "I love you," I said, but he was already sound asleep. And somewhere outside, or in an apartment close to ours, someone was playing The Temptations' "Silent Night" and I closed my eyes and fell asleep to dreams of a golden Christmas angel who granted me my wish.

I want Richard to be happy, and I want to love him forever…

And in my dream, her wings fluttered in dazzling light and she smiled at me. And with a nod, it was done.

CHAPTER TWELVE

RICHARD

I WOKE UP BEFORE GARY. I hadn't taken any pills last night and my leg was reminding me. I was very aware of how many pills I was taking and I didn't want to abuse it, so going one day without wouldn't kill me. I was half-tempted to roll back over and snuggle into Gary again, but it was Christmas morning! I wanted to make it special.

So I quickly got dressed and snuck out of the room. I made eggs and bacon and fresh coffee, and the smell brought a still half-sleeping Kat out of her room. I handed her a cup of coffee. "Merry Christmas."

She blinked and looked up. "Oh, it is! Merry Christmas." She gave me a hug. "This smells amazing. Where's Gary?"

"Still asleep."

"Well, go wake him up," she said. "I'll set the table."

I walked into our room, and I knew I'd have to take an aspirin or something for my leg at some point. Maybe sex last night had been too much, but if all I had to take was an aspirin, I'd count it is a win. There was no way I was abstaining from sex again; I'd waited long enough, and so had Gary.

I sat on the bed. "Hey, sleepyhead," I said, rubbing his arm.

He opened his eyes and smiled when he saw me. "Morning."

"Merry Christmas."

He took my hand and kissed my knuckles. "Merry Christmas."

"I cooked breakfast," I said.

"You did?" he asked, sitting up. "Is that what I can smell?"

"Yes," Kat called out. "Now get your ass out of bed before it gets cold."

Gary laughed, and after he'd used the bathroom, I met him at the table with his coffee. "Thank you, baby."

My cheeks flushed at his words, and Kat groaned as she sat down. "You guys are killing me with the love."

"Well, I'm not even remotely sorry!" Gary said, grinning.

We sat and ate our breakfast, and the chatting and smiles never eased up. Gary made a second pot of coffee, and when all the food was gone, Kat stood up. "I have small gifts for you both," she said. "Shall we sit in the living room? We can clean up breakfast afterward."

"I have something too," Gary said.

They each disappeared into their bedrooms, and I went to the end kitchen cabinet that no one ever looked in. I'd hidden their gifts behind a green glass pitcher and an old tin breadbox that I'm pretty sure my grandmother had once. And when I walked back into the living room, we each stood there with wrapped gifts in our hands.

"I didn't have much money, but I wanted to get you

both something," I said. I gave Kat hers first, then gave Gary his.

Gary kissed my forehead and Kat gave me a teary smile. "You are the sweetest thing," she said. Then she held out a small box to each of us. "For you both."

I took her gift to me and sat on the sofa with my leg outstretched, hung my cane over the armrest, Gary sat beside me, and Kat sat on the floor in front of the Christmas tree. She opened her gift from me. "It's not much," I said, a little embarrassed. "But I thought it was pretty, and it reminded me of you."

She lifted out the necklace and inspected the amber amulet at the end of the long chain. "Oh, Richard, it's beautiful! Thank you!"

"You're welcome. And Merry Christmas."

She got a little teary and slipped the necklace over her head. "Merry Christmas to you too."

Then she opened the gift Gary had gotten her. It was her favorite perfume. "Oh my God, how did you know I was running out?"

"I heard you mumble something about it the other day, and I saw it at the drugstore."

Gary began to open his gift from me. "Maybe you should wait," I said quickly, nervously. "Maybe until we're alone..."

"Is it something of a personal, bedroom nature?" Kat asked with a laugh. "Because I'm not a prude."

I could feel my face turn bright red. "Oh no, nothing like that," I said. "It's just... I don't know what Gary will think..." I cringed. "He might not appreciate an audience."

Gary stopped unwrapping the small box. "Okay. I can wait."

I let out a breath of relief. "But here," he said, handing me my gift. "You can open yours."

"Open mine first!" Kat said. "Then I'll start cleaning up the kitchen and give you guys some privacy."

I lifted her gift for me. It was a decent size box, the wrapping paper had green Christmas trees and candy canes with a red bow, and it made me smile. Inside was a shirt box with two brand new button-down shirts: one blue striped and one solid blue. They looked pricey and very cool.

"I wanted you to have something new and groovy in your wardrobe," she said. "Something to make you feel good when you wear it."

I wasn't sure what to say. "Kat, this is too much! This is more than I imagined and very thoughtful of you, but they must have cost a fortune."

"You deserve it." She smiled warmly at me. "Gary told me your shirt size, but I have the receipts if you need."

"No, they're perfect. Thank you."

Then Gary held up his gift for me. "For you."

I took the box, its paper covered in blue snowmen, and unwrapped it. Inside was a cardboard box that I had to open, and inside that were two silver photo frames. They weren't brand new, but they sure were beautiful. "I thought we could put our photos from Woodstock and Vietnam in them. They'd look great on our dresser or on our bedside tables."

"Gary, they're perfect." The sentiment, how he called everything he owned 'ours' made my heart squeeze.

But in the bottom of the cardboard box was something else. Oh my God. "It's the cigar box from the thrift store," I said, lifting it out.

"Kat told me you had your eye on it."

"I did," I whispered in reply. The box had some

patterned carvings and a little brass latch. It was a handsome piece, and as soon as I saw it in the store, I knew what it would be perfect for. "I thought I could keep all my letters from you in it," I said to him. "That you wrote to me in Vietnam. And maybe my dog tags."

"Oh, Richard," he said, reaching out for my hand. "That's perfect! I wondered what you had in mind for it."

I lifted the lid of the wooden box. "It's been well used, a bit scratched and banged up, but so am I. And I thought that's what made it perfect for my letters. They're my most treasured possession." I shot an apologetic look at Kat. "I mean, the shirts are great—"

She put her hand up and laughed. "Oh, please. If someone wrote me love letters from the other side of the world for a year, they'd be my favorite possession too." She got to her feet and quickly stacked up some plates from the table. "I'll leave you to open your gift," she said with a huge grin and disappeared into the kitchen.

"Can I open it now?" Gary asked quietly.

I nodded. "I just… they seemed like a good idea at the time, but now I'm not sure…"

He was puzzled but undid the tissue paper wrapping to pull out a small jewelry box. He wore an odd smile as he opened it, and I suddenly felt a little ill. "If you don't like it, it doesn't matter. I mean, it doesn't have to mean anything, and the lady at the thrift store gave me a bit of a bargain because I wanted two."

He looked from the two men's onyx signet rings to me. "Why two?"

"One for you and one for me." I swallowed hard. "I know it's probably lame that I bought myself one for your Christmas gift, but it's not like we can walk down the street holding hands or anything, but if we both wear these it'll be our way of showing we're in love without the world knowing, and we'll know what it means but no one else will, and men wear these all the time so no one will think it's queer—"

He slid his free hand around my neck and pulled me in for a bruising kiss, and when he pulled back he was a little teary. "That's the most perfect thing I've ever heard. Richard, that's… perfect." Both rings were similar: a solid silver band with a black onyx square face. They were a little banged up and were hardly flawless, but what they signified was. Gary took the smaller one out, and lifting my right hand, he slid the ring down my ring finger. Then he did the same with his. "Richard," he whispered. "I love you."

"I love you too," I whispered back to him. "Do you like it?"

He shook his head. "No. I *love* it." He looked at his ring, then to me again, then at the ring on my hand. "Merry Christmas, Richard."

He spoke with such love and emotion it made me blush. "Merry Christmas."

Kat cleared her throat, and we both glanced up to see her leaning against the kitchen doorframe. "Could you two be any cuter?"

I fell into Gary's arms and ducked my head, and Gary laughed as he slung his arm around me.

"Dishes are done," Kat said. "I need to get showered and ready to go. I'd ask if you two needed anything, but I think we all know you're not leaving the apartment today."

Gary laughed. "Have a great Christmas with your aunt."

Later after Kat was gone, we each took a shower, and when I came out to the living room, Gary had the mattress off our bed on the floor in the living room in front of the

TV. There were blankets and pillows, snacks, drinks, and lube.

"Make sure the front door's locked," he said with a gleam in his eye.

I slid the latch in place. "Kat definitely won't be home tonight?"

"Nope. Not until tomorrow morning."

"So we have all day."

"And all night."

I held out my hand and showed him the two aspirin. "Do you think we can wait until these kick in?"

"Is your leg sore?" he asked, ducking into the kitchen. He reappeared with a glass of water and handed it to me. "We don't have to do anything. They're showing Christmas movies and cartoons all day long."

I downed the pills and got myself laid down on the makeshift bed. "Oh no, we'll definitely be doing something," I said. "How much lube did you bring out?"

"The whole bottle," he answered.

"That's a good start." I patted the mattress beside me.

Gary grinned and stepped on the mattress, but then he stopped. He walked over to the tree, and taking the Christmas angel, he turned her around so she faced the wall. "Don't want to scare her."

I burst out laughing. "No, we don't. Now get down here with me and do to me all the things you want to do. If I can't walk at all tomorrow, I won't be disappointed."

Gary snorted, but he got himself comfy beside me and pulled the blankets up. We watched TV for all of thirty seconds before his hand began to wander. "Those pills kicked in yet?"

I guided his hand down to my crotch. "It doesn't hurt here."

He chuckled and hummed as he kissed me. "I'm glad to hear that."

He made love to me, with a slow tenderness that left no room of doubt how he felt about me. He was gentle, thorough, and he made sure he met my every need, more than once.

Afterward, I was so sated and so sleepy, we dozed on and off. We watched more TV, we laughed, we ate leftovers from our Christmas Eve dinner, and we made love again.

Gary called his parents, and Pauly phoned us. He'd settled in well at MIT and was living proof that if anyone could convince the genius squad of Boston's mathematical elite to willingly eat hash Christmas brownies, it was Pauly.

By early evening, we ended up showering again, this time together, and when I was completely naked on the mattress in the living room, Gary kissed every inch of me. Even my injured leg.

"Can you feel that?" he asked, kissing one of my dented scars.

"Not on the skin. I can feel pressure, but the superficial nerves are too damaged," I answered. "Or so the doctor said."

He licked across my hip toward my hard-on, smiling, his eyes on mine. "Can you feel that?"

I nodded. "Oh yeah."

So he slipped the head of my cock into his mouth and tongued the frenulum before he pulled off. "And that?"

"God, yes," I breathed. "How can I want more? After all you've done to me today, I thought I'd had enough for a week."

He fisted the base and licked up my length. "This tells me otherwise."

"I want more," I admitted. "I'm so turned on right now, and you feel so good, I never want it to end."

He crawled up my body so he could kiss me. His erection rubbed against mine and it felt sublime, but then he slowly lifted my injured leg, bringing my knee up toward my chest. "Does that hurt?"

"A little, but it's okay."

"I want to make love to you, face-to-face," he whispered. "I want to see it in your eyes when I'm inside you, when you come."

My bones turned to hot mush at his words, and my cock throbbed between us. I certainly couldn't feel any pain in my leg. "God yes, please, Gary."

And when I was ready and when Gary applied enough lube for the both of us, he kissed me and stared right into my eyes as he finally pressed inside me. He cradled my face and watched my eyes as he pushed, inch by inch, into my body. In the most carnal of ways, in the most intimate of ways, he made love to me.

He kissed me, he rocked and thrust, careful of my leg, but taking what he wanted and giving me everything I needed. And I could see it in his eyes too. How good it felt for him, how much he loved me, and how I turned him on.

It was incredible.

He had to keep his weight off me so he didn't put pressure on my leg, and he urged me to stroke myself. "I want to watch you come," he murmured.

I slipped my hand between us and he lifted off me a little, changing the angle of his thrusts. Like he'd found some magic switch inside me, I saw fireworks behind my eyelids. "Oh my God. Do that again!"

So he did, over and over, and I fucked my fist and my orgasm ripped through me —like wildfire, white-hot and uncontained. I came in long spurts, covering my belly and chest, and I felt like I could come for days. And then

Gary's eyes rolled closed. He thrust hard one final time and cried out as he came inside me.

He collapsed on top of me and I relished his weight, his breath at my neck, his pulse I could feel against me, inside me.

He rolled us onto our sides, held me so damn tight in his arms. "I love you," he murmured.

"Love you too," I replied.

"Merry Christmas." His voice was barely a breath.

"Merry Christmas."

"Should I turn the angel back around?"

I chuckled. "Not yet."

Gary propped his head up and gave me a crazy look. "You want more?"

I leaned in and kissed him. "I want it all."

CHAPTER THIRTEEN

GARY

August 5, 1971

TO SAY we'd lived a fairy tale six months would be no exaggeration. It hadn't all been sunshine and roses, but every day we got to live as gay men, true to ourselves, was a damn good day.

After Richard had explained he was nervous about spending New Year's in the city where there would be fireworks and loud celebrations, we took Kat's van to Samuel P Taylor State Park for the weekend.

It wasn't an overly popular destination, and most importantly there'd be no fireworks, so it was perfect. And as it turned out, we weren't the only ones to have the idea. There was another man there named Jimmy who had come back from Vietnam. He'd brought his wife and kids to escape the fireworks as well, and he and Richard got to talking. As it turned out, Jimmy wasn't able to return to his work as a carpenter, but he'd been working a few days a week at a Returned Veteran's office helping others like him. He'd suggested Richard come into the office, and a week later, Richard started two days a week helping returned veterans. Be it as a work placement officer or simply an ear to talk to or a shoulder to lean on, and Richard was loving it.

He was making a difference and he was contributing money for rent and food, and it really gave his self-esteem a much-needed boost. He'd bought a little car—with automatic transmission for his leg—and the added independence helped him tremendously. He still walked with a cane and probably would forever. But he could drive, and he wasn't reliant on anyone else to get him where he wanted.

So when I say the last six months had been like a fairy tale, it wasn't too far-fetched. But that all changed on August fifth.

Everything changed that day.

The government held another lottery draw.

Birthdates were chosen like bingo numbers, only the winner didn't win a door prize. They were drafted into the Vietnam War.

Richard, Kat, and I sat there in our living room and watched in absolute horror as July twenty-fourth was drawn.

My birthday.

We sat there in complete silence staring at the television. Then I could feel Richard's eyes on me, but I couldn't bring myself to look at him. He stood up and walked into our bedroom, and it was then Kat began to cry. "What does that mean?" she asked. "What does that even mean?"

I turned slowly to face her, and I could feel the color drain from my face. "I don't know," I whispered. "I don't know." Then I realized something… "I'm registered through college for those protests, remember?"

"You can't go," she said, more tears spilling down her cheeks.

I shook my head, numb and in total disbelief. "No. I can't. I won't." I swallowed hard. "I just won't go. They can throw me in jail if they have to, but I won't take part in it. I'm not a coward. But I cannot kill another human being. I cannot. I will not hold a gun in my hand for war. For anything. I can't." Panic rose like bile in my throat and tears burned in my eyes. "I've seen what Richard went through, but it's not even that. I just can't… I believe in peace, not war."

Richard walked back out with his duffle bag in his hand and threw it on the sofa. "You're not going," he said. "It'll be over my dead fucking body that this government sends you off to that fucking place."

I looked at his bag, which I realized was now half-packed. "What are you doing?"

"Packing," he answered. His expression was hard and determined. "We're leaving. We can leave now, and we'll be at the border by dawn."

"Canada?" I asked.

"I know a lot of people who've gone. They ask for protection at the border and—"

"They defect?" I got to my feet. "Richard, I don't know if I can leave my country—"

He looked me right in the eye. "You think your country cares about you? Do you think they give a rat's ass whether you live or die? I can tell you, they don't. And if that's not bad enough, if you manage to survive fucking hell on earth, you come home only to get spat on when you walk down the street. No, all you'll get from your country are nightmares that don't go away and a letter that starts with 'On behalf of a grateful nation.' Grateful?" He shook his head and scrubbed a tear from his face and he laughed without humor. "They fucking despise us. They despise me. They have no idea what I went through. What I still go through. I watched men die over there, friends. I can still hear them scream." He took a shuddering breath and more tears filled his eyes. "I can't let you go through that. I won't."

"Richard's right," Kat said, now standing beside us. She put her hand on my arm. "Gary, you can't go to war."

I let my tears fall. "I know. I just can't."

Richard took my face into his hands and wiped a tear away with his thumb. "I love you, Gary. And I'll go to Canada with you. We'll start over there; I have contacts through work. And when the war is over, we can come back."

Finally I gave a nod. What else could I do? Go to jail? I couldn't go to war. I could not in good conscience or with any fiber of my being shoot at people and fight in a war I didn't believe in. I stood for peace and love. I'd literally protested *against* the war, and if I had to choose between being a draft dodger or a killer… well, it wasn't a choice at all.

The phone rang and made us all jump. Kat rushed to answer it and she looked at me with a nod. "Gary. It's your mom."

My poor mother was crying so hard I could hardly understand a single word she said. She'd obviously watched the draft lottery. "Mom," I said through my own tears. "We're going to Canada. Richard and I will be leaving tonight as soon as we're packed. I can't go to Vietnam, Mom. I just can't."

There was silence for a moment, then she managed to contain herself long enough to say, "Good. Oh, thank God, Gary. Yes, please go. Be safe."

We spoke for a little while longer, and she made me

promise to call when we got there and to please, please stay in touch.

I stood there with the phone to my ear, watching Kat and Richard pack up things and bundle belongings into bags, and it felt surreal; like an out-of-body experience. And when I finally hung the receiver into the cradle, Kat came out of the kitchen holding a shoebox. "What about this," she said, taking off the lid. Inside was the golden carved Christmas angel.

"She comes with us," Richard said. "I think we might need her."

Kat gave a hard nod, and within the hour, we'd loaded the last things into Richard's little car and we stood on the sidewalk. Lit only by streetlight, I could see Kat was crying again. She threw her arms around me. "I left some money in the coffee jar," I told her quietly. "To help cover rent until you find someone."

"Thank you," she said, wiping her face with the back of her hand. Then she hugged Richard. "You take care of him."

"I will," he promised.

"Call me when you get there, and be safe. I love you guys," she said and waved us off.

I'll never forget it. It was ten past eight on a Thursday night, the air was warm, the skies were clear, and we were leaving behind the only country I'd ever known. It was the right thing to do, the only thing for me to do, I knew that. And like Richard somehow knew, he reached over and took my hand.

And together, we drove north toward an uncertain future. We had no clue what the next few days would bring, but we had each other, and that right there was worth the fight.

EPILOGUE

JANUARY 21, 1977

Five years later

WE NOW CALLED VANCOUVER HOME. As soon as we arrived at the border seeking permanent residency, Richard phoned his contact with the Vancouver committee that was dedicated to helping Americans, and we were met with open arms.

If I'd thought for one second we'd be alone up here, I was very wrong. There were literally tens of thousands of Americans, just the same as us. Richard basically walked right into a paying job, this time not just helping returned servicemen but also those avoiding the draft and those who wished to start new lives in Canada.

We got an apartment, and just a week or two later, I found work at a telephone company as a business analyst.

And life was good. We called home every so often and Kat had even visited us twice. She'd found herself a new man who wasn't threatened by her brains and drive for her own career, and they'd stayed a few days with us after their honeymoon.

So yes, life was good. It was easy to forget that I'd been labeled a draft dodger.

The war in Vietnam had technically ended almost two years ago, but the truth was, for some people it would never be over. Richard still had shitty days every now and then; completely out of the blue he'd have nightmares or a movie would have helicopters or gunfire and he'd freeze up.

He was getting better. His leg was almost back to normal, and he didn't need his cane anymore, though his limp would become more pronounced if he was tired. He wouldn't be running any marathons, but for the most part, his life was normal.

We'd made good friends here. Our life was here now, and that was perfectly okay with me.

I beat Richard home, so I took Pixie, our three-year-old rescue dog, to the park for a walk. Then I started making dinner when I got back. He still wasn't home, which was a little odd, so I was relieved when I heard his key in the door.

He came into the kitchen and found me chopping veggies. "Hey," I said, leaning over for a kiss. "I was wondering where you were."

He gave my beard a little scratch like he always did. "Have you seen the news?" he asked.

I shook my head. "No, I didn't turn it on. I walked Pixie and thought I'd make a start on dinner." I put the knife down and wiped my hands on the dish towel. "Why? What's up."

He walked over and pressed the knob on the TV. "President Carter just issued a full pardon to all draftees."

I wasn't sure I'd heard him right. "A what?"

"A full pardon. To anyone who fled the country or failed to register." His smile became a grin. "You're now free to go home whenever you want. We can go see your folks!"

My head began to swim. I could see my parents...

"Davey's coming by," Richard said. "He called just as I was leaving the office. He wants to say goodbye."

Davey was a young guy who had left the States the day after his eighteenth birthday. Richard had befriended him the day he arrived, and he lived just one block over. He had dinner with us often—he knew we were a couple—and even though he hadn't said it outright, we were sure he and his buddy John were closer than they let on. There had to be a reason why two younger guys were so comfortable hanging out with an openly gay couple.

Davey was twenty-one now and hadn't seen his family in three years. With brown floppy hair and innocent eyes, he was a sweet kid, and he reminded me a lot of the Richard I first met in that diner all those years ago. I'd miss his smiling face.

"He's going home?"

Richard nodded. "Can't say I'm surprised."

"He misses his family."

"Yeah. He really does." Richard's grin widened. "John's going with him."

"He is?"

"Yep." Richard nodded, and there was a knowing twinge to his smile.

Then right on cue, there was a knock on our door and Richard let him in. Davey patted Pixie first, as he always did. He wore his faded jeans and an old hockey shirt, his hands shoved into his back pockets and a grin on his face. John stood back, a little quieter as he usually was, but smiling nervously.

"Richard says you're going home," I said.

He nodded. "Unconditional pardon," he said. "My mom's driving up from Idaho. I told her I was coming back, and she was already in the car coming to meet me halfway."

That made me laugh. He'd been alone when he arrived, and he missed his family so much. "I'm happy for you."

"Will you go back too?" he asked.

I looked at Richard and smiled. "Our lives are here now."

Richard smiled right back at me. "Yep. We add *U*'s and *S*'s to our words now, and we just need to start watching that stick on ice game…"

"Hockey?"

"That's it," Richard said a wink. "Hockey. Then we'll be true Canadians."

Davey laughed, then he said, "I just wanted to thank you both. But Richard, you in particular. I'd hate to think what would've happened to me if I hadn't met you."

"You're more than welcome," Richard said. "Oh, I just want to grab something. Hold on."

Richard disappeared and we watched him go. "You leaving right now?" I asked. "Don't want to stay for dinner?"

"We can't. My mom is literally already driving to meet me."

I laughed. "Well, be safe."

"I will, thank you. And I mean it, I'm truly grateful for both of you."

"Anytime," I said. "And if you ever come back this way, you make sure you come see us, okay?"

He nodded, and Richard came out holding a familiar shoebox. I knew what he was about to do. "I want you to take this," Richard said. He opened the lid and showed him the Christmas angel ornament. "She'll look after you like she did me. She was given to me after I left Vietnam, when I got out of the hospital. And I can't describe it, but she's special. Like, if you make a wish, she makes it come true."

Davey looked from the angel to Richard, to me, and back to Richard. "For real?"

He nodded and I smiled at him. "It's the truth. Look after her, and when you no longer need her, pass her on to someone else who needs a little help."

"Are you sure?" Davey asked. He gave John a glance and John blushed.

"Absolutely," Richard said. "I got my wish. Now it's your turn."

Davey took the box with a promise to look after it. We wished them both well and made sure Davey had our number. Richard made him promise that if he encountered any issues at the border that he'd call us right away, and with a final round of hugs, we waved them off.

Richard sighed. "They remind me of us," he said.

"I was just thinking that."

"Giving the angel to them was the right thing to do, right?"

"I think it was perfect. We don't need her help anymore, but those two might need a little nudge."

Richard slid his arms around me, rested his head on my chest, and sighed. "I hope so." Then he pulled back. "You never did tell me what you wished for that very first Christmas."

I laughed and gave him a kiss. "And I won't tell you now."

"Was it about me?"

"Of course it was."

"I told you I didn't make a wish," he said with a glint in his eye.

"You told me you thanked the angel instead."

"And that was kind of true." He shrugged. "But I did wish for something."

"Shhh," I said, kissing him so he'd stop talking. "Don't tell me or it won't come true."

"It already has." He smiled serenely. "It was about you. And forever."

I chuckled and kissed him again. "Pretty sure that's what I wished for."

"This Christmas, we'll have to find a new angel for the tree."

"New angel, new wishes."

He made a thoughtful face. "Nah. My wish has been the same every year. I don't see it changing any time soon."

"Mine neither. Just you and forever. That's all I'll ever need."

The End

About the Author

N.R. Walker is an Australian author, who loves her genre of gay romance. She loves writing and spends far too much time doing it, but wouldn't have it any other way.

She is many things: a mother, a wife, a sister, a writer. She has pretty, pretty boys who live in her head, who don't let her sleep at night unless she gives them life with words.

She likes it when they do dirty, dirty things… but likes it even more when they fall in love.

She used to think having people in her head talking to her was weird, until one day she happened across other writers who told her it was normal.

She's been writing ever since…

Also by N.R. Walker

Blind Faith

Through These Eyes (Blind Faith #2)

Blindside: Mark's Story (Blind Faith #3)

Ten in the Bin

Point of No Return – Turning Point #1

Breaking Point – Turning Point #2

Starting Point – Turning Point #3

Element of Retrofit – Thomas Elkin Series #1

Clarity of Lines – Thomas Elkin Series #2

Sense of Place – Thomas Elkin Series #3

Taxes and TARDIS

Three's Company

Red Dirt Heart

Red Dirt Heart 2

Red Dirt Heart 3

Red Dirt Heart 4

Red Dirt Christmas

Cronin's Key

Cronin's Key II

Cronin's Key III

Exchange of Hearts

The Spencer Cohen Series, Book One

The Spencer Cohen Series, Book Two

The Spencer Cohen Series, Book Three

The Spencer Cohen Series, Yanni's Story

Blood & Milk

The Weight Of It All

A Very Henry Christmas (The Weight of It All 1.5)

Perfect Catch

Switched

Imago

Imagines

Red Dirt Heart Imago

On Davis Row

Finders Keepers

Evolved

Galaxies and Oceans

Private Charter

Nova Praetorian

Titles in Audio:

Cronin's Key

Cronin's Key II

Cronin's Key III

Red Dirt Heart

Red Dirt Heart 2

Red Dirt Heart 3

Red Dirt Heart 4

The Weight Of It All

Switched

Point of No Return

Breaking Point

Starting Point

Spencer Cohen Book One

Spencer Cohen Book Two

Spencer Cohen Book Three

Yanni's Story

On Davis Row

Evolved

Free Reads:

Sixty Five Hours

Learning to Feel

His Grandfather's Watch (And The Story of Billy and Hale)

The Twelfth of Never (Blind Faith 3.5)

Twelve Days of Christmas (Sixty Five Hours Christmas)

Best of Both Worlds

Translated Titles:

Fiducia Cieca (Italian translation of Blind Faith)

Attraverso Questi Occhi (Italian translation of Through These Eyes)

Preso alla Sprovvista (Italian translation of Blindside)

Il giorno del Mai (Italian translation of Blind Faith 3.5)

Cuore di Terra Rossa (Italian translation of Red Dirt Heart)

Cuore di Terra Rossa 2 (Italian translation of Red Dirt Heart 2)

Cuore di Terra Rossa 3 (Italian translation of Red Dirt Heart 3)

Cuore di Terra Rossa 4 (Italian translation of Red Dirt Heart 4)

Natale di terra rossa (Red dirt Christmas)

Intervento di Retrofit (Italian translation of Elements of Retrofit)

A Chiare Linee (Italian translation of Clarity of Lines)

Spencer Cohen 1 Serie: Spencer Cohen

Spencer Cohen 2 Serie: Spencer Cohen

Spencer Cohen 3 Serie: Spencer Cohen

Confiance Aveugle (French translation of Blind Faith)

A travers ces yeux: Confiance Aveugle 2 (French translation of Through These Eyes)

Aveugle: Confiance Aveugle 3 (French translation of Blindside)

À Jamais (French translation of Blind Faith 3.5)

Cronin's Key (French translation)

Cronin's Key II (French translation)

Au Coeur de Sutton Station (French translation of Red Dirt Heart)

Partir ou rester (French translation of Red Dirt Heart 2)

Faire Face (French translation of Red Dirt Heart 3)

Trouver sa Place (French translation of Red Dirt Heart 4)

Rote Erde (German translation of Red Dirt Heart)

Rote Erde 2 (German translation of Red Dirt Heart 2)

Thank you for reading

A Soldier's WISH

N.R. WALKER